Juliana looked up, her parted. "She moved."

"The baby?" Jason eased closer.

"Yes, I'm sure that's what it was. The doctor said I might feel something soon—like the flutter of a butterfly's wing. And I just did."

His hand lifted. "Can I...?"

"Yes, of course. But I'm not sure if it's strong enough for you to feel anything yet."

He placed his hand on her tummy, felt the swell of her womb, the warmth of her body, the softness of her breath. And although he couldn't feel any movement whatsoever, he didn't draw away. He just stood there, caught up in her floral scent and in the intimacy of the moment.

* * *

BRIGHTON VALLEY COWBOYS: This Texas family is looking for love in all the right places!

Dear Reader,

Welcome back to Brighton Valley and to the Leaning R Ranch, where the Rayburn heirs are struggling to sort out the family heirlooms, as well as deal with the memories they each had there.

The first book is Jason Rayburn's story. The eldest of three children who share the same father but have different mothers, Jason is up to his elbows dealing with corporate problems, as well as dividing up his late father's estate. When he hires Juliana Bailey to help him inventory and pack up the furnishings of the Leaning R Ranch for an estate sale, the lovely redhead stirs up more emotions in him than the long-forgotten memories of the old house in which he grew up.

In Juliana's arms, he finds the one thing he's been missing his entire privileged life. But does he dare give his heart to a woman carrying another man's baby?

If you like family secrets, you're going to enjoy this new Brighton Valley series. So pour yourself a glass of iced tea or your favorite drink and find a comfy spot to curl up with a new book.

Happy reading!

Judy Duarte

PS I love hearing from my readers. Feel free to contact me through my website, judyduarte.com, and let me know what you thought of this story. I hope you enjoy reading it as much as I enjoyed writing it.

The Boss, the Bride & the Baby

—

Judy Duarte

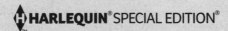

Recycling programs
for this product may
not exist in your area.

ISBN-13: 978-0-373-65903-6

The Boss, the Bride & the Baby

Copyright © 2015 by Judy Duarte

Printed in U.S.A.

Since 2002, *USA TODAY* bestselling author **Judy Duarte** has written over forty books for Harlequin Special Edition, earned two RITA® Award finals, won two Maggies and received a National Readers' Choice Award. When she's not cooped up in her writing cave, she enjoys traveling with her husband and spending quality time with her grandchildren. You can learn more about Judy and her books at her website, judyduarte.com, or at facebook.com/judyduartenovelist.

Books by Judy Duarte

Harlequin Special Edition

Return to Brighton Valley

The Soldier's Holiday Homecoming
The Bachelor's Brighton Valley Bride
The Daddy Secret

The Fortunes of Texas: Cowboy Country

A Royal Fortune

The Fortunes of Texas: Welcome to Horseback Hollow

A House Full of Fortunes!

The Fortunes of Texas: Southern Invasion

Marry Me, Mendoza

Byrds of a Feather

Tammy and the Doctor

Brighton Valley Babies

The Cowboy's Family Plan
The Rancher's Hired Fiancée
A Baby Under the Tree

The Fortunes of Texas: Whirlwind Romance

Mendoza's Miracle

Brighton Valley Medical Center

Race to the Altar
His, Hers and...Theirs?
Under the Mistletoe with John Doe

Visit the Author Profile page at Harlequin.com for more titles.

To Betsy Bramblett, a dear friend and fellow author.
I enjoy our times together.
Let's have coffee again soon!

Chapter One

Jason Rayburn had never considered himself an early bird, but as the morning sun began to rise over the Leaning R Ranch, he found himself pouring his second cup of coffee.

If his father hadn't died, he'd be in Houston today still in bed, most likely, but with thoughts of hitting the gym instead of repairing the barn door. After a good workout, he'd take a shower, then head to the downtown high-rise he owned and take the elevator to the top-floor office of Rayburn Energy Transport, where he was the founder and CEO.

With the recent death of his father, he now controlled Rayburn Enterprises as well, not to mention his new role as the sole trustee of the Charles Darren Rayburn Family Trust.

What a mess dividing *that* was going to be. And that's what had led him back to Brighton Valley.

The Leaning R had been part of his great-grandmother's estate, rest her soul. And Rosabelle Rayburn had left it to Charles with a stipulation—that it be divided equally to his issue upon his death. She'd wanted his children to be in complete and wholehearted agreement about its daily operation and/or division.

Yeah. Right. Jason and his half siblings had never been in agreement on anything. Granny, of all people, knew that. And he suspected it was her last-ditch effort to draw them together in a way she'd never been able to do while she was alive.

But there'd been a reason for that. Jason, Braden and Carly had so very little in common they might as well be strangers.

So that's why he had to get the Leaning R up and running again and ready for sale. Because there was no way his brother and sister would make good business partners. He just hoped he could get them to agree on a real estate agent and a price.

When Jason was a kid, spending summers and the occasional holiday at the ranch, he'd dreamed of being a cattle rancher. But those days were long gone. He was a busy CEO now.

On rare occasions those old dreams might come back to haunt him, but there was a reason for that. He'd spent enough time on the Leaning R with Granny Rayburn growing up that he'd actually felt more at home here than he had anywhere else. Of course, that wasn't the case anymore. He was a city boy now—and eager to get back to his life in Houston.

He didn't have time for reminiscing, especially when some thoughts were so bittersweet they could make a grown man actually choke up like a little boy. Yet as he walked through the house, assessing the work that needed to be done, the still-lingering scents of lemon oil and Granny's trademark lavender hand lotion assailed him in every room. So it was nearly impossible to escape the memories.

But he wouldn't allow himself to lollygag in the past. He had too much to do, and he was determined to get the hell out of Dodge, so to speak, as quickly as he could. In the meantime, he'd set up a home office to work remotely. The corporate world didn't stop spinning just because he had to handle some family business.

He would have to hire a couple of extra ranch hands to help Ian, the foreman, get things done. But that didn't mean he wouldn't have to work along with them. He didn't mind the physical labor. It actually drew him back to the time when his great-grandma was still alive, when he was a boy who loved to ride the fence line with the cowboys who'd worked on the Leaning R.

Too bad Granny wasn't here to fix him silver-dollar pancakes for breakfast or to tell him about more of Grandpa Dave's escapades.

He glanced at the faded blue wallpaper with pictures of straw baskets holding wildflowers. Now yellowed with age, the colors had once brightened Granny's kitchen.

Damn, but he missed that sweet old woman. She'd been the closest thing to a mother he'd ever had.

The coffeepot gurgled, and he took one last sip of his morning brew before dumping the remainder in the sink. It wasn't Starbucks, but at least it was caffeine.

He glanced at the cat-shaped clock on wall, its drooping black tail swishing back and forth with each tick-tock. Time to get moving. He had a lot to accomplish today.

Headlights flashed through the kitchen window, and tires crunched on the gravel drive as a vehicle pulled into the yard and parked. He wasn't expecting anyone this early, but it wasn't as if this was the Wild West and he needed to protect his homestead.

Looking out the kitchen window, he watched a woman climb from the small pickup, her hair pulled into a topknot. Instead of heading for the front door, she went straight for the back entrance—just as though she owned the place.

Carly?

His half sister had said she'd come out and help him inventory the household furnishings for an estate sale—the most difficult part of the job, which he had yet to face. But he hadn't been expecting her until tomorrow. What was she doing here now—and at the crack of dawn? She'd never been an early riser, at least not that he could recall.

Jason was already in the mudroom when the door swung open and Carly stepped inside.

"This is a surprise," he said. "You're a day early. Want some coffee?"

"No, thanks. I can't stay."

"What's going on?" he asked.

"I just got offered a singing gig—an important one—and I have to leave town for a few weeks. But I wanted to let you know that there are some boxes in the attic that Granny was keeping for me. I don't want you to throw them out or sell them. That's why I agreed to help you inventory things, especially since I think you're being way too hasty in selling the ranch."

He knew how she felt. But it made no sense to keep the Leaning R going when there was no way the three of them could work together. And he had enough on his plate already.

"You could let Braden run things," she added.

Hell, he and Braden rarely spoke. How in the world were they supposed to be business partners? That was one reason he was in a hurry to get the estate settled— so the three half siblings could each go their own ways. Not that he wouldn't keep in touch with Carly. But with her heart set on singing and acting, that just went to show that they had nothing in common except the DNA they'd inherited from their old man.

"I also have some things to drop off for Braden," Carly added, "but since he's not home, I'm going to leave them here for him to pick up."

"What are you talking about?"

"Braden asked a friend to drop off some stuff with me. I've had it a week, but I'm leaving and already gave notice at my place. So I don't want him to worry about where it is if he needs it."

Jason kept in closer contact with Carly than he did

their half brother. When they'd been kids, Jason had blamed Braden for the divorce that had sent his mom into an emotional tailspin. Of course, as he grew older, he realized Braden had been as much a victim as he'd been. But you couldn't fix a relationship that had never really developed.

"Slow down," Jason said. "Where is Braden?"

"I'm not sure. I think he's in Mexico. It was all pretty cryptic. His friend pretty much just dropped the painting off, along with a couple of boxes. He said it was important that I keep it for him."

"Why can't you leave it at Braden's ranch?"

"There must be a reason why he wanted me to hang on to it. Braden's supposed to explain more when he comes to pick it up. He said he'd owe me one—but now he'll owe you."

Jason was about to object, but it wouldn't hurt to have his half brother indebted to him, even if none of this made any sense. "Did he say when he'd be back?"

"As soon as he can, apparently. A few weeks at the most."

"What the hell? I want to get this property listed for sale. I can't be away from my office while you and Braden are out traipsing around and going on with your lives. It's not fair. And who's going to help me pack up all this stuff?"

She blew out a ragged breath. "Talking to you is just like talking to Dad. I knew you'd never understand."

Her words struck like the flat of a hand against his cheek. For as long as Jason could remember, he'd been trying to win his dad's approval, by following in his footsteps, by attending the same college, becoming a business major, starting his own company. Yet he'd never meant to become a carbon copy of the man.

"Try me," he said.

She merely rolled her eyes—big and blue, just like her mother's.

Jason didn't blame her for being skeptical. He and Carly had never been particularly close. For one reason, at twenty-four, she was six years younger than he was. She'd also been into music and the arts, while he'd been more interested in sports and, later, getting his MBA.

But since the three half siblings would have to compromise during the division of the estate, a task that seemed nearly impossible considering they couldn't figure out a way to be in town at the same time, it was imperative that they learn to find some kind of common ground.

"Tell me about your singing gig," he said.

She unfolded her arms and cocked her head slightly to the side, studying him as though she'd never met him before. Then she slipped her thumbs into the front pockets of her jeans, rocked forward and smiled. "I'm starring in a nightclub near the Riverwalk. It's a six-week run, but it could work into something bigger— *better*."

She made it sound as if she'd been asked to star on Broadway.

So what would it hurt for him to pretend that she had?

"That's great, Carly. I hope things work out for you."

She paused a beat, then tucked a loose blond curl

behind her ear. "So you're not going to fight me about storing Braden's stuff while he's gone?"

He hoped that didn't mean holding off the sale longer than he'd planned, but if he really thought about it, his relationship with his half brother was in far more need of repair than his and Carly's. And if that meant doing Braden this favor now, then how could he refuse?

"Can you stick around until I find someone else to help me go through the household items?" he asked.

"I'm afraid not. I start tonight, and I have to get back to San Antonio for a wardrobe check this afternoon. It's a long drive."

Crap. How was he supposed to go through the house on his own, plus supervise the ranch work—and hold down the fort at Rayburn Energy, as well as Rayburn Enterprises, without help?

Besides, he'd been hoping Carly would agree to go through the household items. It was hard for him to do it. Everything he saw, everything he touched, reminded him of Granny, and…well, it was hard. Damn hard. And Carly would know better than he would what should be kept and what should be tossed or sold.

"I'm going to have to find someone to help," he said. "And quickly. If they can live in, then all the better."

A slow grin stretched across Carly's face, and he was struck by how pretty she was, even without any makeup. She'd always favored her mother, a popular country-and-western music star and who'd retired recently to marry a state politician. But he hadn't realized how much until now.

"I know someone who'd be perfect—and she's looking for work."

"Who?"

"Remember my friend Juliana Bailey?"

Red hair, pigtails. Big brown eyes and a scatter of freckles across her nose. "The one I used to call Bird Legs? What about her?"

"She's been working in Wexler at an art gallery since graduating from the junior college, but she was laid off recently. Now she's back in town and waiting tables part-time at Caroline's Diner. But she needs to find something that pays better. I'm sure she'd do a great job. And maybe, if you were happy with her, it might work into something more permanent—and in the city. I know she'd love to find something outside of Brighton Valley."

"I wouldn't want to give her any false hope about working at either Rayburn Energy or Enterprises. I leave the hiring up to the HR department. It makes my life a lot easier if I don't get involved with the personnel. But I definitely need some temporary help here on the ranch, and I'd be willing to make it well worth her time."

"You won't be sorry. Juliana is bright, professional and…well, whatever it is HR departments are looking for in new hires. I'm not sure why that company in Wexler let her go. They'd have to be crazy or going out of business, because she had to be their best employee ever."

"You don't have to sing her praises. I'm a little desperate right now."

"Good. I think she's working this morning. I don't have her new number, but you could stop by Caroline's and talk to her. I know she's been staying with her mom and grandmother in a small apartment near Town Square, so she'd probably work for room and board and a fair salary."

Seriously? "You think she'd be interested in a simple offer like that? Even if it's only temporary?"

"Well, that and the opportunity to at least have a chance at an interview with the HR department at one of your businesses. It wouldn't hurt to ask."

"Okay, I will."

"Thanks, Jason. You won't be sorry."

For some reason, he was sorry already. But he set his mug on the counter and followed Carly out to the yard, catching up to her about six feet from the pickup. "How many boxes are there?"

"Two—one containing some ceramic stuff and another with paperwork. There is also a painting." She opened the tailgate, then reached for a box. "Here. Can you carry this one into the house?"

Jason took the carton she handed him, although he had half a notion to drop the damn thing on the ground—or take it and dump it off at Braden's ranch, which was ten miles down the road.

"Have you tried calling him?" Jason asked as he and Carly carried the boxes back into the house.

"Several times, but apparently he doesn't have cell reception wherever he is."

"Didn't you think to ask what he was doing down there?"

"Braden's not much of a talker."

That was the truth. And he certainly wasn't likely to confide in Jason. Hell, they kept each other at arm's distance as it was. And as much as Jason would like to change that—as much as he now *needed* to change that—he couldn't very well build or repair their relationship all by himself.

They deposited the boxes on the kitchen table, then returned for the paintings. He was supposed to be documenting all the stuff in the house so they could get rid of it—not adding more clutter. If he wasn't so determined to mend his relationships with his siblings, he'd…well, he wasn't sure what he'd do.

But damn his father for dying and leaving him with a dysfunctional family and a messed-up estate to complicate his life when he had his own business issues to deal with.

And damn Braden for being so secretive and only making things worse by going MIA when his family needed him most.

Before he could voice any further objections, Carly was behind the wheel of her red Toyota pickup and heading down the road just as dawn broke over the Leaning R.

Now what?

He might as well head into town and get breakfast at Caroline's. He needed some help, and it appeared that he was going to have to snag Caroline's newest employee away with a better offer—room, board, a small salary and the hope that something better might be in the cards for her.

He didn't want to even consider what he'd do if she didn't accept his offer.

For a woman who'd once thought she'd left small-town life behind, Juliana Bailey seemed to have re-turned to Brighton Valley with her tail between her legs. Not that anyone knew that yet.

As far as the small-town rumor mill went, she'd been laid off at her job at an art gallery in nearby Wexler and had moved home to the two-bedroom apartment her mom and grandma shared above the drugstore. She currently slept on the sofa bed and made the short, one-block walk to Caroline's Diner, where she'd picked up part-time work at a job destined to only last a few more days—at best.

She had a game plan, though. And that was to get out of town before her secret came out. In the mean-time, she held her head high and bustled about the diner with her order pad in hand and wearing an oversize apron that matched the yellow gingham café-style cur-tains in the windows facing the street. She'd always been fashion conscious, but not as of late.

Loose blouses and an apron tied above the waist hid a multitude of sins, namely a growing baby bump, a secret that would be impossible to keep much longer.

Thankfully, no one other than her obstetrician, Dr. Selena Ramirez-Connor, knew that she'd been deceived by a man who'd neglected to tell her he was married. But if she wanted to protect her mom, who happened to be a church secretary, and her grandma, who worked at city hall, from her scandal, she'd have to get out of Brighton Valley quickly.

Trouble was, Juliana had just moved into a nicer place near La Galleria in Wexler, and when she'd decided to leave town, she'd had to use her savings to get out of her lease. So she didn't have enough left to move to the city, especially since she didn't have another job lined up yet. And with a baby due in five months… well, she was strapped right now.

As she refilled the coffee of the lone diner at table three, an elderly gentleman with thinning hair, she caught a whiff of greasy sausage swimming in the runny egg yolks on his plate. Her tummy swirled like a mop in a slop bucket, and for a moment she thought she'd have to have to run to the restroom.

She blinked her eyes and swallowed as the brief bout of nausea passed.

For the most part, the morning sickness that had plagued her for nearly six weeks straight had ended. But there were still a few random moments, like this one, when she wasn't so sure…

"Thanks, hon," the diner said. "I don't s'pose you have any of those caramel cinnamon rolls left, do you? Margie said they were made special yesterday, and I was hopin' to have me another today."

"I'll check and see. If they're gone, I can get you one of the oatmeal spice muffins."

"Sure, that'll do."

Juliana had no more than turned from the table when the bell on the front door jangled, alerting her to a customer's entrance. She didn't normally give the arrivals much notice because Margie, the other waitress, was quick to greet the many diners who flocked to Caroline's for the food as well as the local gossip.

And the news that passed quickly from one person to the next, helped along by Margie, was another reason this was a bad place for Juliana to work if she didn't want to bring any undue embarrassment upon Mom and Grandma.

But for some reason, Juliana glanced at the doorway now, only to note a stranger. Well, not exactly a stranger, but a face she hadn't seen in years.

Jason Rayburn—who else could it be?—had grown up and filled out in the manliest way.

He was tall—six foot or more—with dark hair that was stylishly mussed. Even though she'd heard the wealthy exec was staying in Brighton Valley, she hadn't expected to see him dressed in faded denim and a chambray shirt. It almost made him appear to fit right in, when he was as far from one of the locals as a man could be.

She'd followed his success and found him somewhat intriguing. Actually, the entire Rayburn family was pretty newsworthy around here—including both Carly and Braden. Maybe that's why folks found them interesting. They had the same father, but they couldn't be any more different.

She knew Carly and Braden well. Jason, though, was more of a lone wolf. A wealthy and successful one, from what she'd heard.

He'd gone into business with his father right after

college. And he'd rarely come back, except for Granny Rayburn's funeral. But he'd left town nearly as quickly as he'd come in.

He scanned the small diner. When his eyes zeroed in on her, a smile stretched across his handsome face, creating a pair of dimples and sparking a glimmer in his green eyes.

As he sauntered toward her, as lean as a cowboy and as cocky as a man used to staking his claim on just about anything he had a mind to, she nearly dropped the coffee carafe.

"Well," he said, flashing a boyish grin and sending her heart rate topsy-turvy, "if it isn't Bird Legs."

She couldn't help but return his smile. "If I remember correctly, I threw a rock at you the last time you called me that."

"Yes, you did. I'd been bad-mouthing my brother, Braden, and you felt the need to stick up for him. And if I recall, you missed me by a mile."

"That's true, but I scared your horse."

"Thankfully, I'm a good rider."

That he was, although the mare had gotten skittish and Juliana had been sure he was going to get thrown. But she hadn't liked him picking on Braden, who'd been her friend and sometime riding buddy.

She lifted the glass carafe, which bore more brown stain than coffee. "I'm brewing a new pot. If you'd like to grab a seat, I can pour you a fresh cup."

"Sounds good. Thanks. Which tables are yours?"

He wanted her to be his waitress? Okay. Why not?

She nodded toward the yellow-gingham curtains. "Any of those by the window."

"All right."

She retrieved a menu, as well as a fresh pot of coffee, and took them to him. "Here you go." After upturning the white mug on the table in front of him, she filled it. "Cream or sugar?"

"Just black."

"Okay. I'll give you a minute to decide what you'd like, then I'll come back."

"Thanks. It won't take me long."

She felt his eyes on her back as she returned the carafe to where it belonged. Yet she feared there was more heat radiating from his stare than the coffee warmer.

Margie, who'd worked at the diner for as long as Juliana could remember, sidled up next to her and snatched the carafe labeled decaf. "Isn't that Jason Rayburn?"

"Yes, it is. I talked to Carly not long ago, and she said he's staying out at the Leaning R while he's getting it ready to sell."

"That's what I heard." Margie was up on all the local gossip, whether it was accurate or not. "But he's grown up since I last seen him, so I hardly recognized him. He doesn't favor Braden much, does he? But he does have the look of a womanizer."

"Why do you say that?" Juliana asked.

"Looks too much like his daddy to not be. And you know what they say. The apple doesn't fall far from the tree."

Charles Rayburn had grown up on the Leaning R

with his paternal grandparents, but it had been his maternal grandfather who'd paid for his college and who'd set him up in business. At that point, he'd pretty much left Brighton Valley in the dust. Or so they said.

"I'd better get his order." Juliana stepped away from Margie and made her way back to where Jason sat near the window.

The morning sun cast a glare on the dull brown Formica tabletop, but it had nothing on the sunny smile Jason tossed her way when she asked, "What'll it be?"

"Huevos rancheros. I haven't had that in ages."

"You got it." But instead of turning and walking away, she took a moment to bask in the glimmer of those meadow-green eyes. What color would a city girl call them?

Enough of that now. She had to get over her fixation on a palette of colors ready to spring to life on a blank canvas. She'd have to postpone her dream of becoming an artist.

And a romance gone bad made any other fantasies out of the question, too. So she returned to the kitchen and placed Jason's order. As much as she ought to keep her distance, she had a job to do.

"Can I refill your coffee?" she asked when she passed his table a few minutes later.

"Yes, thanks." He eyed her for a moment, as though assessing her.

Was he considering how much she'd changed? Did he like what he saw? Again, she chastised herself for letting her thoughts veer in that direction, even though it seemed only natural to wonder as his gaze caressed her face, her hair, her eyes.

"Carly told me you were working here," he said.

"Just a couple days a week. I was laid off at the art gallery in Wexler and plan to find work in Houston. This is just a temporary position to help tide me over until I find something permanent in the city."

"Well, I'm glad you were working today."

The way he continued to study her made her wonder if he'd come in just to see her—and not to order breakfast. But she quickly dismissed the idea. "I'm glad I was here, too, Jason. It's nice to see you, again. How long has it been? Ten years?"

"Something like that."

She smiled and nodded toward the kitchen. "I'll check on your breakfast."

Fortunately, Caroline was just placing his plate on the counter. So Juliana picked it up, along with a couple of warm flour tortillas and a small dish of butter. Then she placed his meal in front of him.

"Did my sister tell you I was staying out at the Leaning R?" he asked.

"She mentioned it."

"Did she tell you why?"

"She said you plan to sell the place." And that she wasn't any happier about the decision than Braden was. But Juliana knew enough to keep that to herself.

"I also need to inventory everything and get it ready to sell. It's a huge job, and I need to hire someone to help me. Carly mentioned that you might be interested in the position."

"That depends." Juliana definitely needed the extra money.

"If you're talking about the pay, I'd make it worth your time."

She placed a hand on her tummy, a movement that was becoming a habit, then let it drop. In truth, she was thinking more about the time it would take for her to get the job done. She only dared spend a few more weeks to a month in the area before her baby grew too big to hide. "What do you have in mind?"

"Can you take a leave of absence from here? I'd need you full-time for about three weeks."

She wasn't even working four hours a day as it was, and she suspected Caroline had only offered her the position as a favor to her grandma.

"I'd be willing to pay you a thousand dollars a week," Jason said.

Her pulse rate shot through the roof, and she struggled to keep her jaw from dropping to the floor. That was more money than she could expect to make anywhere. And it would certainly help her relocate to Houston and give her time to find another position.

"There's a guest room at the ranch," he added. "You can either commute each day or stay there, if you'd like. Whatever you're comfortable doing. But it's going to take a lot of work and time. Granny was sweet as can be, but she wasn't very organized."

Not that Juliana wanted to stay out at the ranch with Jason, but the sooner she got out of her mom's house and away from downtown Brighton Valley, the better her chances were of keeping her pregnancy secret.

Still, she was torn about accepting the offer. After all, the man's father had had a reputation for loving and leaving the ladies, which meant Jason might not be honorable, upright or honest. And she'd just gotten out of a relationship with a man like that.

Besides, what would the townspeople say if they thought she was shacking up with Jason out at the Leaning R?

But the generous salary he was offering her was too tempting to ignore.

Besides, if things worked out and she proved herself handy and competent, he might recommend her for an office position at Rayburn Energy in Houston, which would be her ticket out of Brighton Valley for good—and before word of her fall from grace got out into the rumor mill.

All the reasons she ought to turn him down ping-ponged in her brain. She'd fallen for a womanizer's lies and didn't want to cross paths with another one. And as Margie had said, the apple didn't fall far from the tree.

But the money he was offering her would allow her to leave town sooner and give her time to find another position in Houston.

"So what do you say?" he asked.

"When do you want me to start?"

Chapter Two

Jason had barely returned to the Leaning R and gone though a couple of cupboards when his office called with a list of several critical issues he needed to handle. He dealt with each one, which took no less than an hour.

When a pause sounded on the line, he realized that the last crisis had been averted—for the time being, anyway—so he adjusted the cell phone pressed against his ear, sat back in his desk chair and blew out a sigh. This was why he needed extra help on the ranch. He couldn't run a company and get the place ready to sell, even if he could get his siblings to agree. Not by himself.

"By the way, Mr. Rayburn," Marianne, his executive assistant, said, "we received a billing from a company called DII, which stands for Discreet International Investigations. They're charging over three thousand dollars in services, plus fifteen hundred in expenses."

Jason stiffened. "What in the hell was that for?"

"From what I understand, it's a private investigation firm that did some research for your father in Mexico about four months ago. Braden had them send the bill to the office and told me that it was a legitimate expense."

"Who gave Braden the right to authorize a payment like that?" And even more importantly, why had his father hired a PI? Did that have anything to do with his reason for being in Mexico when he died?

"I'm not sure, sir. That's why I didn't want to forward it to the accounting department without running it by you first."

"Thanks, Marianne. Put a hold on it for now. I need to check into this." After the line disconnected, Jason called his brother's cell phone. The unusual ringtone indicated Braden was still in Mexico, but he didn't answer.

For the next couple of hours, Jason continued to sort through cupboards while stopping every so often to try his brother's number with no success. By the time a car drove up and parked near the front of the house, he was madder than hell and ready to fight at the drop of a hat.

Funny how just being in this house had him lapsing into the Western vernacular. He'd be saying "Howdy" and "y'all" if he didn't get back to the city soon. He glanced out the window, only to spot an attractive red-head climbing from a white Honda Civic.

Juliana.

His frustration dissipated as he left his work in the kitchen, as well as the mess he'd strewn about the living room, and met her on the front porch.

An attitude change wasn't so difficult once he saw her face-to-face, though. How did a woman become prettier in a matter of hours?

She'd shed her apron, for one thing. And she looked a lot less frazzled, for another. Maybe that's because he was seeing her in the light of day instead of the diner.

The afternoon sun glistened off the gold strands in her copper-colored hair, which hung loose about her shoulders. Her eyes, a caramel shade of brown, glimmered under a fringe of long, dark lashes. She still bore a light scatter of freckles across a turned-up nose. But in a most attractive way that made a man want to memorize each one.

She wore a cream-colored gauzy top, and while it wasn't the least bit formfitting, he found it sexy in a feminine way.

Rounding off her ensemble was a pair of shorts and sandals that revealed neatly manicured toenails.

"I'm glad you're here," he said, his gaze traveling up—taking in her pretty face, then tempted to travel back down again.

Damn, get a grip. He was glad to have her here. He needed the help. But he didn't need her to realize that she'd also brought in a ray of sunlight to what had started out as a dreary day.

"Here," he said, "let me take your bag."

"It's not heavy."

"Maybe not, but for some reason, I've been doing quite a bit of reminiscing these past few days. I think it's a side effect of being here at the ranch. And I can't help but hear Granny's voice urging me to remember my manners."

"Then by all means," she said, handing over her suitcase while hanging on to her purse and a small canvas tote bag. "I wouldn't want to disappoint her."

His movements stalled for a moment, long enough for Granny's voice to hover in his memory. *You're a good boy. You know right from wrong, Jay-Ray. Don't disappoint me like your daddy did.*

But he shook it off as quickly as it came. He'd done his best to make both his great-grandmother and his father proud. Trouble was, he wasn't so sure he'd pleased either one.

He led Juliana through the living room, winding through the mess he'd made, and into the hall. He'd thought about giving her one of several guest rooms, but decided upon Granny's bedroom, which was bigger and had a private bathroom.

"I thought you'd be more comfortable in here." He placed her suitcase on the lavender floral quilt that draped the queen-size bed.

"Thank you. This will be fine." She set her purse and the tote alongside her bag. Then she glanced around the room, which he hadn't entered in years — until he'd come in last night to change the sheets, dust and air things out.

He wasn't sure why he hadn't come into Granny's room before then. Too many memories, he supposed. Even the furnishings, the white eyelet curtains, the embroidered throw pillows, still held a whiff of Granny's powdery lavender scent. It was enough to draw a boy farther inside—and to make a man withdraw.

Juliana walked toward the south wall, which displayed a gold-framed portrait of Granny that appeared to be fairly recent. She'd only been gone for three years, and it couldn't have been painted too long before that.

"That's a perfect likeness," Juliana said. "She looks just as I remember her—the eyes, the nose, the smile."

Jason followed her, taking note of the expression that had been caught on canvas and thinking the same thing. "It's like looking at a photograph, yet it's softer. And almost real."

"Did she have it commissioned?"

"I assume she did. I don't remember seeing it before last night." But then again, he hadn't been home for any notable visit in years.

"The artist is quite talented." Juliana stepped closer and read the signature in the corner. "I used to work in a gallery, but I've never heard of Camilla Cruz. I don't believe she's local."

That was odd. Then where had Granny met her? Jason supposed it didn't matter, so he shrugged it off. "I'll tell you what. Why don't you unpack and freshen up. Afterward, you can meet me in the den—I've set up a temporary home office in there. It's two doors down on the left. As soon as you're settled, we can go over your job assignment."

"Sounds great. I won't be long."

True to her word, Juliana only took a few minutes to put away the clothing and toiletries she'd brought with her. Then she met Jason in the oak-paneled room with a bay window that provided a view of the front yard and the big red barn.

He had an all-in-one laser printer, fax and scanner that took up a table near a built-in bookshelf on the far wall, as well as a laptop computer that sat next to an old-style PC with a big, bulky monitor that had been outdated years ago.

"I see you brought your own office setup."

He glanced up from his work and smiled. "I tried to talk Granny into updating her computer system a couple of years ago, but she refused. My dad bought it for her about fifteen years ago and installed it. She'd gotten so used to that dinosaur that she couldn't see parting with it. But I need something a lot more high-tech for what I do."

She nodded then moved into the den. "So where would you like me to start?"

He glanced at the laptop screen and clicked the mouse, just as the printer roared to life. "I created a spreadsheet to inventory the items inside the house. If you make a note of them on paper first, we can input the data into the computer afterward. Some of the items are antiques, so we may need to research their value."

"What about the sentimental value?"

He looked at her as if she'd uttered words in a foreign language. "Carly mentioned that. I suppose some people are more prone to form emotional attachments to things like furniture, but I don't. And I doubt my brother does, either."

"You're wrong." She bit her lip, wishing she could take it back. She hadn't meant to be so judgmental, even if she had wanted to defend Braden. "I'm sorry, it's just that I don't think you know your brother very well."

Again he paused for a beat. "You're right about that—Braden and I haven't been close. And if you grew up here in Brighton Valley and heard the local gossip, then you probably know why."

Not for a fact, but she was aware of the rumors. And Braden had said enough to allow her to come to a few conclusions of her own. Their father, Charles Rayburn, had been married to Jason's mother when he'd had an affair with Braden's mom, during which Braden had been conceived. Jason's mom had sued for divorce, but for some reason, Charles had never married Braden's mother.

"Your family connection may not be one of your own choosing," she said, "but you're brothers just the same. I'd think that would account for something, especially after having that relationship for more than twenty-five years."

"Believe it or not," Jason said, "I'd like things to be different between us."

"Have you told Braden that?"

"If we could find time to spend an hour or two

together, I probably would." He got up from his seat, crossed the den, pulled the empty spreadsheet from the printer and handed it to her. "This is pretty self-explanatory."

Okay, so he was done discussing his feelings about his brother. That was fine. It wasn't any of her business anyway. So she scanned the document and nodded. "When do you want me to get started on this?"

"Now, I suppose."

"Do you plan to break for dinner?"

He glanced at the clock on the desk. "I guess we'll have to. Sometimes I forget the time and work until my stomach growls, but that's not fair to you."

"Would you like me to cook something?" she asked.

"That wasn't part of the deal, but sure. If you don't mind. You may have to hunt and peck to find something decent to fix, though. I have some lunch meat and sandwich fixings, but I haven't done any real grocery shopping."

"I'll see what I can come up with."

"We can trade off kitchen duties," he added. "But on my nights, we'll probably call out for pizza. I'm not much of a cook."

"That sounds fair to me." She tossed him a smile, then headed for the kitchen.

Before she stepped foot into the hall, he stopped her. "I have a question for you."

She turned and waited in the doorway.

"How do you know Braden so well?"

"We were neighbors before my grandma's ranch went into foreclosure. He and I used to be riding buddies back then. I guess you could say we were friends and confidants."

He merely studied her for a moment, as though he found that difficult to believe. Or maybe as if he might be a bit envious.

But of whom? Her or Braden?

From the way those meadow-green eyes were boring into her, she couldn't be sure.

Juliana set out a delicious, mouthwatering spread of tuna rice casserole, sliced tomatoes, homemade biscuits and Granny's canned peaches. Jason sat in awe at her domestic capabilities, especially when she didn't look the least bit like a homebody.

She'd probably meant to keep her long, wavy red hair out of the way while she'd cooked, because now she wore it in a sexy topknot, with wisps of escaped curls dangling along her neck and cheeks. He would have guessed that she might have done it on purpose to tempt him—if she'd also changed out of that attractive gauzy blouse and put on a slinky tank top instead.

But she hadn't. She'd also kept on that pair of knee-length shorts that revealed shapely calves. While they were modest and a far cry from a revealing pair of Daisy Dukes, there's no way he'd ever call her Bird Legs again.

Now they stood at the sink, washing the last of the dishes, a chore he'd always done while staying on the Leaning R and seemed especially fitting this evening.

"Did I tell you how much I enjoyed dinner?" he asked.

"Yes, several times. And you're welcome—again." She tossed him a dazzling smile. "But I'm going to have to go shopping tomorrow to pick up something from the meat market. There wasn't much to choose from, other than the sandwich fixings you had in the crisper, tuna, biscuit mix and your great-grandmother's canned goods."

"Those peaches were a real treat. And I can't remember the last time I had tuna. To be completely honest, I might have passed if it was offered on a menu. But it was actually really good. Where did you learn to cook like that?"

"My mom taught me. She's a whiz at making a meal out of whatever she can find in the pantry."

Jason rarely talked about his past, but for some crazy reason, he found himself saying, "You're lucky. I lost my mom when I was just a kid."

"How old were you?"

"Ten."

"I'm sorry. At least you were old enough to have some memories of her."

Not too many good ones. The years he'd spent living only with his mom hadn't been all that happy. She'd been emotionally broken and damaged by his father's cheating.

When he'd eventually gotten a stepmom and was able to move in with her and his dad, Carly's mother had been too busy with her singing career to stay home with her own baby, let alone with a boy who wasn't hers. So Jason had been sent off to an elite boarding school.

But that was okay. It had been good for him. Everyone had said so. Everyone except Granny, anyway. He'd once overheard her tell his father what a mistake he was making. But when that summer was over, he was sent right back to Thorndike Prep as always.

Still, he did have those vacations...

Thankfully, Juliana didn't ask a lot of questions, and Jason was glad. He'd never been comfortable with anyone expressing their touchy-feely emotions or expecting him to talk about his own, especially when it came to his mother.

Granny had tried to step in and take on a maternal role, but it wasn't the same. Hell, his mother hadn't even been a real mom. He supposed he was one of those kids who'd pretty much grown up on his own in a lot of ways. He just hadn't been without any of the essentials or all the shiny extras—houses all over the place, private school, fancy cars...

But he didn't want to think about any of those lonely days and crappy memories, not when he had a beautiful woman at his side. So he said, "I have a bottle of merlot in the pantry. How about a glass of wine?"

"I'd rather have a glass of juice, if you don't mind. And under the circumstances, let's call it a debriefing. We can also create a game plan for tomorrow—or set up a calendar for trading off meal duties. But to tell you the truth, I don't mind cooking. I'm not fond of cleaning up, though."

If he was being honest with himself, as well as with her, he'd rather create a game plan for *tonight*, complete with romantic music, maybe a slow dance under the stars. But Juliana had put a stop to that by setting them both back on track. And he ought to thank his lucky stars that she had. Sexual harassment training was a priority for everyone in upper management at Rayburn Energy, and he'd best keep that in mind.

He offered her a platonic smile—his best attempt at one, anyway. "You're right. That's what I meant. Grab two goblets, then make yourself comfortable on one of those chairs on the porch. I'll get the wine and juice."

Moments later, he took the uncorked bottle of wine and a quart of orange juice outside. After filling their glasses, he took a seat, joining her under the soft yellow glow of the porch light.

He took a sip of his merlot and glanced at the barn door with the chipped paint and broken hinge that dusk couldn't hide. He'd have to ask Ian McAllister, the foreman, to fix that next. Then they'd have to paint it, along with the corral nearest the house.

Juliana glanced out onto the ranch, which still needed so much work to be the kind of place Granny had called home, a ranch she'd be proud of if she were still alive.

He tried to look at the family homestead through Juliana's eyes. He was going to have to hire more hands than Ian to help out around here. It was going to take an army to get it back into shape, even though they had only a handful of cattle left in the south forty.

So why hadn't he recruited those extra men yet? Why was he dragging his feet?

"What are you going to do with the Leaning R?" Juliana asked.

"Granny wanted me, Braden and Carly to run it as three equal partners, but I can't see how we can do that." Jason reached for the bottle of juice and replenished her glass. "Unlike most siblings, Braden, Carly and I never agree on anything—the food we eat, the clothes we wear, the books we read."

Even their memories of childhood and Daddy Dearest were as different as the three women who'd given birth to them.

Since Jason was the only one who didn't have a mother, he'd been closer to their father. Not that he and his dad had done any of the usual father-son activities, like playing catch or going camping. His father had been way too busy with his corporate obligations.

Interestingly enough, they both attended charity functions benefiting the Boys Club and other youth programs, to which Charles and Jason both contributed financially. It was, he supposed, the closest they came to having a typical relationship. But Jason wouldn't complain. He shared more with his dad than either Carly or Braden did. And while he hadn't cried when he'd gotten word that his father had died in a car accident in Mexico a few months back, he'd still grieved.

Jason and Juliana sat quietly for a while, lost in the night sounds on a ranch that had seemed like a ghost town when Jason had arrived last week.

When he'd driven up that first day, there hadn't been any cattle grazing in the pastures along the road, no Australian heeler named Mick to greet him. The barn, once painted a bright red, had weathered over the years and was in such disrepair that instead of asking Ian to take care of it, he'd thought he probably ought to hire a carpenter or two.

But it wasn't until he'd noted the boarded-up windows on the house, unlocked the front door and entered the living room that the old adage struck him and he had to agree.

You really couldn't go home again.

Whenever he'd visited the Leaning R before, he'd always expected to catch the aroma of fried chicken or roast beef or maybe apple spice cake—whatever Granny had been cooking or baking that day. But this time he'd been accosted by the musty smell of dust and neglect.

The first thing he'd done was to pry the boards off the first-floor windows and let in the morning sun. Then he'd called a cleaning service out of Wexler to put the place back to rights—or at least, as close to it as possible.

Jason had only spent school breaks and summer vacations on the Leaning R, but it had been his one constant. And the one place that held his warmest childhood memories.

Still, his plan was to put it on the market before summer was out—if he could get both Carly and Braden to sign the listing agreement. He hadn't expected an argument from Carly, but he'd gotten one. And he expected one from Braden—whenever the erstwhile rancher finally showed up. Then again, he'd never been sure about anything when it came to his half brother. The two of them were only three years apart, but they'd kept each other at arm's length for as long as Jason could remember.

Granny had tried to encourage a friendship whenever Braden came to visit, which was usually on Christmas or holidays. But Braden had a mother and family of his own. Maybe that was why Jason sometimes resented him coming around.

Either way, Granny couldn't create a closeness between the brothers that wasn't meant to be.

But why stress about any of that when he had pretty Juliana seated beside him?

He took another sip of merlot, savoring the taste.

"So what're your plans after this?" he asked. "What's next for you?"

"I'm going to get a job in the city—Houston, maybe."

"Not Wexler?"

"No." The word came out crisp, cool. Decisive.

Hmm. Bad memories?

She'd been laid off, Carly had said, and was only back in Brighton Valley temporarily.

Financial problems? Bad investments? Taken advantage of by a con man? Or maybe a lover?

It was too soon to ask. Still, he couldn't help wondering.

Either way, Wexler's loss was his gain. Or so it seemed, especially when he was sitting outside with a beautiful woman and finding even more solace under the stars.

There was also a lovers' moon out tonight, casting

a romantic glow over the Leaning R. His hormones and libido were pumped and taunting him to make more out of their time on the porch than a quiet chat, but common sense wouldn't let him.

Juliana had made it clear that she didn't want to cross any professional boundaries. What if she quit and left him alone to deal with the mess by himself?

He stole a glance at her, and when he caught her looking his way, she quickly averted her gaze. But as his attraction and interest continued to build, he realized it wouldn't take much for him to reach out and touch her.

Or, at the very least, to ask her why she was adamant about not returning to Wexler.

Juliana hadn't meant to stare at her employer, but he'd been so deep in thought that she couldn't help it.

Okay, so she hadn't just noted the intensity in his furrowed brow. She'd also been checking out his profile and the way his hair appeared to have an expensive cut, yet was stylishly mussed. In that Western wear—the worn jeans and chambray shirt rolled at the forearms—he looked like a Texas rancher. And a handsome one at that.

She tried to imagine him in a designer suit, seated at a board meeting in a high-rise building that looked out at the city skyline. He surely had to be quite impressive. Either way, Jason Rayburn was the kind of man who could turn a woman's head.

He'd certainly turned hers. But she didn't dare let her attraction get out of hand.

"Would you like some more OJ?" he asked.

"No, thank you. I've had plenty already." In her condition, she had to use the bathroom a lot more than usual. And after all the orange juice she'd had already, she'd be lucky if she could make it through the night without waking at least once.

"This probably isn't any of my business," he said, "but do you mind if I ask you something?"

She'd always been fairly open and up-front, although she'd learned to be a lot more cautious recently. "It depends on what you want to know."

"I get the idea you'd like to relocate. I can see why you might want to live in a bigger city. But I also sense that you couldn't leave Wexler fast enough. And that it might be due to bad memories."

She stiffened and leaned back in her chair. Her hand slipped protectively to her tummy. Instead of removing it, which she did whenever she'd found herself doing so in public, she opted to let it linger in the yellow glow of the porch light, allowing her baby the loving caress it deserved. "You're right."

"About the bad memories?"

"That the reasons aren't ones I want to share."

Silence stretched between them like a balloon she'd blown too full. Just before the tension popped in her face, she added, "But yes, there are some bad memories, too."

"Related to your employment?"

The man didn't quit, did he? She turned to him, caught his eyes drilling into hers. Why the sudden inquisition? Shouldn't his questions about her background and previous employment have come up earlier?

Did she owe her new employer, albeit a temporary one, an answer to that line of questioning?

Maybe and maybe not. But a brief yet truthful response might help to quell his curiosity and put this awkward discussion to rest.

"Yes and no," she said. "But if it eases your mind, I didn't lie or steal. And when I left on my last day at work, my personnel file was unblemished. I wasn't fired or laid off, though. I actually quit. If they have any complaints about me as an employee, it's that I didn't give a proper notice."

He nodded, and before he could quiz her any further, she added, "Just so you'll feel better about hiring me and trusting me with your family business, I had a romance that went south rather suddenly, and I wanted to put as much distance between the two of us as I could. Brighton Valley is just a pit stop before I take off for good."

"I'm sorry," he said.

"About my breakup?"

"About quizzing you and making you feel uncomfortable. But for the record, I'm actually glad you left the guy and his memory behind."

A slight smile tugged at her lips, but she tried to tamp it down. All she needed was to lower her guard to the point of doing or saying something she'd regret. And if she'd learned anything out here in the moonlight, she was going to have to stay on her toes around a man like Jason Rayburn.

If he were like his brother, it wouldn't be an issue. She knew Braden as well as she knew anyone in Brighton Valley. His mother's family had been ranching in these parts for years. His grandfather was on the town council for a while. And his mom was involved in the women's auxiliary at the Wexler Community Church. He came from decent people. In fact, she often wondered what his mom had ever seen in his father—especially if what she'd heard about Charles Rayburn was true.

In spite of herself, Juliana risked another glance at Jason, watched him take a drink of his wine, then stare out into the night sky, where a full moon and a splatter of stars glistened overhead.

But the stars weren't the only things sparking. Her pregnancy hormones were surely coming into play and had to be triggering unwelcome romantic thoughts, which were totally inappropriate. She blamed it on her recent betrayal, the stillness of the evening and, yes, maybe a growing attraction.

For all those reasons, she couldn't continue to sit outside with him tonight. It could only lead to trouble—or at the very least, temptation.

She had a job to do—one that paid better than could be expected. And she intended to make the best of it.

Even if she didn't land an interview or a possible position with Rayburn Energy or Rayburn Enterprises, she could use a good recommendation, because she wasn't likely to get a very good one from the gallery.

In fact, after the details of her romance and breakup became known within local art circles—and they certainly could have by now—she knew better than to ask for any kind of reference at all.

Chapter Three

Juliana had lost track of how many sheep had jumped over her bed that night—surely a flock that would make a Basque sheepherder rich.

Blaming the two goblets of orange juice she'd drunk while on the porch with Jason for her need to get up every couple of hours, she gave up the struggle for sleep just after midnight. She remembered reading somewhere that warm milk might help, but there wasn't any in the refrigerator. Chamomile tea was another option, although she didn't recall seeing anything like that in the pantry.

A trip to the market was definitely in order, especially if she was going to do any more cooking while she was on the Rayburn ranch. Since she was wide-awake, she figured she might as well head to the kitchen and start a grocery list.

With that in mind, she rolled out of bed and pulled her robe from the closet. She didn't bother with slippers. As she took a moment to stroke the slight bulge of her womb, she pondered the phrase *barefoot and pregnant*.

How fitting was that?

As she opened the door, she noticed the light on in the den. Had Jason forgotten to turn it off when he went to bed?

She padded down the hall. When she turned into the doorway, she spotted him seated at the desk, glaring into the screen of his laptop. She studied him for a moment.

He'd run his fingers through his hair numerous times this evening. Yet even mussed, it didn't appear the least bit scruffy. Compliments of a highly paid stylist, no doubt.

He frowned as he stared at his laptop, his brow furrowed. Yet even the intensity of his expression didn't take away from his appeal.

She had no idea how long she stood there gazing at him, admiring his handsome profile, as well as his work ethic. A couple of minutes, she supposed.

Finally, he looked up and noticed her watching him in the doorway. "I'm sorry. Did I wake you?"

She smiled. "I never really went to sleep. What are you doing?"

"Problem solving. At least, that's what I'm trying to do. We're working on a marketing strategy that hasn't been coming together for us, and I've been racking my brain to figure out what's missing."

"I wish I could help."

"So do I, but the best brains at Rayburn Energy, including the head of the marketing department, haven't been able to agree on the best layout." He pushed away from the desk. "I'm not sure if I should put on a pot of coffee or call it a night."

"I'd think caffeine is the last thing you need right now."

He tossed her a boyish grin. "You're probably right. Too bad we don't have any ice cream or cookies."

"I'll put dessert on my grocery list. That is, if you want me to do any shopping for meals tomorrow."

"I hadn't thought that far ahead, but now that you mention it, I suppose we'll have to find time to eat during the day. I don't mind calling out for food, but if you want to pick up groceries, that's fine with me."

"We can play it by ear. But I'll whip up something for dinner tomorrow." She glanced at the clock and smiled. "Make that tonight. So what'll it be? Chocolate or vanilla?"

"If you're talking ice cream, let's go with rocky road. I like nuts."

"I'll keep that in mind as I start that list." She reached for the black leather cup on top of the desk that held pencils and pens. "Do you have any paper?"

He took a pad that rested near the laptop and handed it to her. "Here you go." Then he returned his gaze to the screen that had him so perplexed.

"Can I take a look at it?" she asked. "Maybe I can help."

Jason bit back a smile, which had been better than

the chuckle that almost slipped out. The problem had stymied experienced execs with MBAs. Juliana had no experience in the business world.

Okay, so she'd worked as a sales clerk at an art gallery in Wexler. But still, she didn't have the background that would provide her with the experience or the expertise she needed to actually know what she'd be looking for.

But what the hell.

He rolled back his chair, making room for her to see the screen. Then, using the mouse, he showed her the latest artwork and the graphics the marketing department had sent him earlier this evening.

"I see what you mean," she said. "Something's definitely missing. It doesn't have any spark."

She had that right. And while everyone knew something was missing, no one seemed to know quite what that something was.

"I think," she said, "if you merged the wording of number three with the graphics of number four, then used the background of number one, it would be a lot closer to what you're looking for."

"Maybe so," he said. "I'll give that some thought. Thanks."

As she stood beside him, he caught a whiff of her scent—something soft and exotic. He wasn't sure what he'd been expecting her to be wearing. Something down-home and country, he supposed. Something more suited to Brighton Valley. But then again, she was city bound. Why wouldn't she have a more sophisticated air? But did her scent come from her perfume or lotion? Or perhaps from her shampoo?

He glanced at her wild, bed-tousled curls, which gave her a sexy look that the frumpy cotton robe couldn't hide.

What a contradiction she seemed—country vs. city. Lady vs. vixen.

Once again, his attraction built to the point he found it impossible to downplay or ignore, especially at this late hour, with several bedrooms down the hall to choose from.

Unable to help himself, he reached out and twined a loose red curl around his finger. "Has anyone ever asked you if your hair color is real?"

She sucked in a breath, yet she didn't pull away. "Yes, they have. And it is."

"I know it's real. I remember you when you were a girl. It's just that the shade is so…remarkable. Most people might question whether it was possible for something that pretty to be natural."

Their gazes met and locked. For a moment, he could have sworn their breathing stopped.

Then she took a step back, and as her hair tightened against his finger, he let it uncoil.

While he might have released their physical connection, something else held them taut. Something he could almost reach out and touch.

She bit down on her bottom lip, then placed her hand over her stomach. He'd seen her make that nervous gesture before, which seemed to be unique to her. Other women nibbled a nail or twisted a strand of hair around a finger seductively. But he'd never seen another stroke her belly.

He found it kind of cute—the gesture, as well as the fact that he made her nervous.

She took another step back, clearly uncomfortable with the heat sparking between them, and nodded toward the doorway. "I'm going to start that grocery list now. And then I'll try to get some sleep. Otherwise I won't be worth a thing tomorrow."

He sensed that she was the kind of woman who'd be worth her weight in gold—either as an employee or a lover. But he damn well couldn't have her as both. So he let her go.

As he heard her bare feet pad down the hardwood floor, he glanced back at the screen, which displayed the artwork the head of marketing had sent him. He tried to imagine the changes Juliana had mentioned, realizing they did have some merit.

The woman might not have a business background, but she did have some experience with art—if you could give her points for working at what had to be a two-bit gallery in a town that wasn't much bigger than Brighton Valley.

After giving her suggestion some thought, he shrank the screen and signed into his email account.

Doug,
Do me a favor. Try using the background on number 1. Then merge the text of sample 3 with the graphics on 4. Let me see what that looks like.
Jason

Then he hit Send. He wasn't an artist, so he'd have to see the sample to know if it would work the way Juliana seemed to think it would. But it certainly sounded as though it might be a lot closer to what they were looking for.

If that was true, Juliana would have more than paid for her keep already. Of course, it was early yet. They still had a ranch full of memories to pore through.

And less than three weeks to do it.

In spite of getting very little sleep last night, Jason woke early and started breakfast. By the time Juliana walked in, freshly showered and ready to start the day, the coffee had finished brewing and the bacon sizzled in Granny's favorite cast-iron skillet.

"Something sure smells good," she said. "I thought you weren't a cook."

"I'm not, but I was a Boy Scout. So some things are easy. But I'm usually better frying bacon on a campfire." He tossed her a smile. "I'm also good at making s'mores."

She laughed, which lent a flush of pink to her cheeks and lit a glimmer in her caramel-colored eyes.

Damn, she was pretty—even casually dressed in blue jeans and a blouse she hadn't taken the time to tuck in, the bottom button still undone.

"Besides," he added, "I didn't want you to think that you were going to starve while living out in the boondocks. And the truth is, I'm pretty good at fixing breakfast."

"That reminds me," she said, "I'll need to make a

grocery run sometime today. That is, unless you want to do it."

He reached into his pocket, withdrew his wallet and peeled out several hundred dollars. "Will this cover whatever you have on the list you made?"

"That'll be more than enough." She folded the bills in half, then tucked them into the front pocket of her jeans. "My plan is to get started with the inventory and packing. Then I'll take a break and go to the market sometime this afternoon."

"That sounds good to me." He nodded toward the coffeepot. "It just finished brewing. Would you like a cup?"

"No, thanks. I'll finish the orange juice instead."

He pulled the OJ from the fridge. Then he emptied the carton into a glass he withdrew from the cupboard and handed it to her. "You'll have to add juice to that list."

"Will do." She turned and moved about the kitchen, taking time to check out the scarred oak table and chairs, as well as the various plaques, pictures and cross-stitch hangings with upbeat sayings Granny had used to adorn the walls.

Jason hadn't wanted to spend any more time in this room than he had to. If he wasn't careful, it would be too easy to become nostalgic and reflective here, mostly because he could almost feel Granny, could still hear her speaking to him, especially with so many of her favorite sayings nearby.

He glanced over his shoulder at Juliana. She was looking closely at a decoupage plaque. He couldn't actually read the words, but he knew what that one said. It was a Bible verse.

He hadn't meant to memorize it, but for some reason, it had stuck with him for years and he'd never forgotten it. He probably never would.

Granny had pointed it out to him the day before he'd left for prep school in California. She'd said she had claimed that particular proverb as God's promise to her. For that reason, she said that she knew Jason, unlike his father, would grow up to be his own man. And that he'd always choose to do what was right and true.

For a moment, Jason thought Juliana might read it out loud. She didn't, though. Yet she didn't have to. He could almost hear Granny saying it to him again. *Train up a child in the way he should go, and when he is old he will not depart from it.* Proverbs 22:6.

Still, Juliana continued to study it, as if pondering the wisdom of it.

"Did you know my great-grandmother?" he asked.

Juliana turned to him and smiled. "Just about everyone in Brighton Valley did. She was a warm and caring woman. I think she was a lifetime member of the PTA, even though she hadn't had a child in school for ages. She was also very involved in the Brighton Valley Community Church. When my mom was recovering from surgery, she and a couple other ladies brought meals to the house on a regular basis."

"What about when Granny was sick? Before she died. Did anyone from the church bring meals to her?"

"I'm not sure. As far as I know, she kept her illness to herself."

Jason certainly hadn't heard a peep from her about any ailments. But then again, she'd never been one to complain. Her doctor must have known something, though. "You don't think she told anyone how sick she was?"

"No, I don't think so."

Still, her family should have been aware of it. And they should have done something—visited more. At the very least, one of them should have been with her at the end so she didn't have to die alone.

A stab of guilt shot through him. Had she thought that her family hadn't come through for her like they should have?

More importantly, had she thought Jason hadn't?

Sure, he'd called regularly and sent money. He also had made a point to come to visit on Christmas and her birthday. Not always on the actual day, but close enough to count.

At least, he'd always thought so. But now, standing in her kitchen, surrounded by her furnishings, by her memory, he wasn't so sure.

Juliana moved on to the far corner of the kitchen, where Jason and Carly had set the boxes and the painting that belonged to Braden.

"What's this?" she asked. "Did you get sidetracked and leave this stuff here?"

"Actually, that can stay where it is. It belongs to my brother. He's supposed to come for it when he gets back from Mexico."

She reached for the painting, a Southwestern style of an old church at night, with a crescent moon and bright stars overhead.

"This is very good," she said.

"Yes, I suppose you're right. But I've never been a huge fan of that particular style. I do like the bright colors, though. It would look good in a ranch-style home."

That's probably why Braden had bought it. Jason returned his focus to the bacon, removing the last strip from the pan and turning off the flame.

"Wow," Juliana said. "That's weird."

Jason turned and leaned his hip against the kitchen counter, the tongs still in his hand. "What is?"

"It was painted by Camilla Cruz."

At that, he set the utensil down, turned away from the stove and made his way across the kitchen to the oak table, where Juliana had placed the painting to get a better look.

"The same artist who did Granny's portrait?" Jason asked.

"Yes. The signature is the same. See?"

He leaned in closer to take a better look at the script. "That's really strange."

"I wonder who she is."

So did Jason. Obviously, Granny and Braden both knew her. Or at least one of them did. "Maybe you were wrong about her not being a local artist."

"I suppose she could be," Juliana said.

She seemed to think that she was an art expert, but

Jason wasn't convinced. After all, she'd only worked at a gallery in a relatively small town—and for just a couple of years at most. She was lovely, though.

As she leaned closer, her head angled next to his, her exotic scent snaking around him, he was willing to concede any credentials she wanted to claim.

She glanced closer at the delicate script of the signature. "It's a Hispanic surname. Do you think it has anything to do with why Braden went to Mexico?"

"No, I doubt it. This is Texas. A lot of people have Hispanic surnames. I'm sure Braden is in Mexico because he's following my dad's trail."

Juliana straightened, taking her scent with her.

"Are you sure my brother never mentioned anything to you about where he was going or why?" Jason asked.

"Sorry. I haven't talked to him lately."

Jason glanced at the box of pottery, as well as the other box that had been sealed shut with packing tape. If his brother had been missing in Mexico, with foul play suspected, he would have had every right to tear into the cardboard lid and try to solve the mystery of Braden's whereabouts. But as far as he knew, his brother was alive and on some international escapade, the details of which he'd either neglected or flat-out refused to share with Jason.

And the fact that he was so completely out of the loop didn't sit well with Jason at all. And it only seemed to make the chasm between the two brothers deeper than ever.

* * *

"Are you going to make me eat dinner alone?"

Jason glanced up from the work he'd spread all over the desk in the den and to the doorway, where Juliana stood, her red curls swept into a sexy topknot.

Yet as his gaze traveled from her pretty hair and face to her kissable lips, his eyes and his hormones were thwarted by one of Granny's full-size aprons, a red-checkered background printed with green apples.

If there was something to be said about Juliana Bailey, she was certainly an unpredictable novelty. Yet the contradictions she presented still drove his libido crazy.

"Aren't you hungry?" she asked.

She was talking about food, and while she had him thinking about a different kind of hunger, he realized his stomach had been empty for hours. "Yes, I guess I am."

"Good. I set a table out on the back porch. I decided you need to get outside for some fresh air. You've been cooped up in the house all day."

So she'd taken it upon herself to look after him, huh? "What time is it?"

"Nearly seven o'clock. And definitely time for a break. Something tells me that if I didn't keep an eye on the clock, you'd continue to work until your stomach put up a fuss."

A grin stretched across his lips. "Isn't that how most people know when it's time to eat?"

"I suspect those who get ulcers do, but I have a little more self-awareness than that. Have you always been like this?"

"As far as I can remember."

"Even as a kid? Were you the last one to come in at night for meals?"

His smile deepened as he recalled the days when he'd lived on the Leaning R. "Granny used to have to ring an old cowbell."

"What about after you left the ranch? Who reminded you to eat then? Who took care of you?"

His smile faded. "The cafeteria workers at prep school—and the other staff. Mostly I was lucky enough to fend for myself."

She tossed him a skeptical smile, then rose and headed to the kitchen, the apron bow hanging along her swaying hips and taunting him until she disappeared out the door.

Maybe he hadn't always done the best job of hiding his needs or his loneliness as a kid, but he'd grown up and he'd survived. All in all, it had been for the best, because that's how he'd learned to become strong and self-sufficient.

He shut down the laptop, tidied up his files, then headed down the hall. Moments later, he caught the whiff of a familiar aroma. At least, he thought it was. If he didn't know better, he'd think that Granny was whipping up a batch of her Swedish meatballs.

Before Juliana could remind him to go outside to the table she'd set, he followed the smell to the kitchen, where he found her standing in front of the stove and preparing to spoon the meal from a pot into a serving bowl.

"What are you doing?" he asked.

She turned and smiled, her golden-brown eyes glimmering. "I found some of your great-grandmother's old recipes this morning, and while thumbing through them, I saw that she'd made notes on them." She lifted the worn and stained card that had been resting on the countertop. "This one says, 'Jason's favorite. Serve with noodles and green beans.' So I checked in the pantry and made a list of everything else I would need to surprise you."

She certainly had.

"This is amazing," he said. "*You're* amazing. I don't know what to say."

She smiled and turned completely around, her back to the stove and countertop. "You don't have to say anything."

But he did. And a simple thank-you wasn't enough. Employees often bought him a bottle of scotch or bourbon for Christmas. A lover might buy him an expensive dress shirt and silk tie. Or maybe tickets to a show *she'd* been wanting to see. But no one ever had gone out of his or her way to surprise him in such a heartwarming way. No one except Granny, anyway.

The fact that Juliana had no reason to do it stroked something deep inside him, and without any conscious thought, he closed the gap between them.

As his gaze locked on hers, his expression must have been pretty intense because she asked, "Is something wrong?"

"No, not at all." He'd just realized that her beauty went far deeper than her flaming hair and golden-brown eyes.

When they were just inches apart, he reached up and ran his knuckles along her cheek. Her breath caught, yet she didn't flinch.

"This is one of the nicest things anyone has done for me in a long time," he said.

She offered him a crooked grin, as if trying to downplay her thoughtful gesture. "You haven't tasted it yet. I might have missed a step or skipped an ingredient. It probably won't taste at all like you remember."

"It's the thought that counts."

She didn't step back, but then again, he supposed she couldn't, because he had her backed up against the counter. She brushed a loose curl from her brow, broke eye contact and gave a little shrug. "I just did it on a whim. It was no big deal."

"Maybe not to you, but it feels like a big deal to me."

At that, he snagged her gaze again, and whatever it was that drew him to her seemed to be affecting her the same way, because her lips parted.

And for some crazy reason he might regret later, he lowered his mouth to hers.

Chapter Four

The minute their lips met, Juliana knew she should turn her head and push Jason away. Yet she couldn't help herself and leaned forward and accepted his kiss as if she didn't have a care in the world.

How could she form a single thought, or voice a protest, when her head was spinning from the scent of his woodsy cologne and the sweet taste of his breath as his mouth opened and his tongue sought hers?

When his arms tightened around her and his hands slipped up and down her back, he nipped at her bottom lip, and she all but melted into a puddle on the floor.

Within a heartbeat, the kiss exploded with a passion she hadn't expected, and her common sense—what was left of it—scrambled to take control of her addled brain.

Jason Rayburn was her employer, for goodness' sake. And even if the two of them were willing to overlook that simple little fact, there was another little something she'd better not overlook—a little *someone*.

She splayed her hands on his chest, felt his heart pounding under her fingertips as she pushed against him. Then she finally turned her face and tore her lips from his.

Her ragged breath betrayed her conscience when she tried to offer an explanation for why she'd let him kiss her in the first place, not to mention allowing it to go. "I'm sorry. I don't know what I was thinking. That was completely inappropriate."

"You're probably right, but you have to admit, it was pretty nice."

"Maybe so, but I don't want you to get the wrong idea." She nearly tacked on *about me*. But she left it off, figuring he could make whatever leap he wanted. That he was wrong about her, about what the kiss might mean, about where any of this might be headed.

A boyish grin slid across his face. "I agree that we probably shouldn't get involved, but there's definitely some strong chemistry going on between us."

She took a step to the side, putting more space between them than the counter at her back allowed. "We have a lot of work to get done in a short period of time. So we need to stay on track."

"You're right." He studied her for a beat, then turned toward the stove. "Dinner smells delicious. Would you like me to set the table?"

She ought to be relieved that he seemed to have

put the kiss behind him so easily, but it left her a bit uneasy—and maybe even envious, since she wasn't sure she could do the same thing.

And she'd been right. All during the meal, she'd fought the urge to study the man seated across from her.

As he dug into the Swedish meatballs and noodles, he complimented her several times, completely glossing over the amazing kiss they'd shared just minutes before. Yet here she sat, her cheeks still warm and no doubt flushed.

But just because she'd been swept away momentarily by the unexpected kiss didn't mean she would let it happen again—or that she'd complicate her life with a man right now.

Jason had no more than dished up a second helping of meatballs over noodles when he said, "You have no idea how much I appreciate you fixing this meal. It was always my favorite—and one I never expected to taste again. To thank you, I'd like to take you out to dinner on Saturday night. There's a little Italian restaurant that just opened up downtown. I'm not sure how it's going to compete with Caroline's Diner, but it's only open for dinner. And it's probably a little too fancy for most of the Brighton Valley locals."

"You don't owe me anything." Juliana lifted her napkin and blotted her mouth as if she could block her thoughts from coming out. Surely, he wasn't asking her out on a date. But that had to be what he was doing. Hadn't he listened to a word she'd said? She didn't want to get involved with him—or with anyone.

Of course, neither did she want to jeopardize her temporary job—and a lucrative one at that—by putting up too many flashing red lights and roadblocks, especially when she'd kissed him back in a way that could only have been taken as a full-on green light. No wonder he sensed a contradiction.

"I'm afraid all my clothes have been packed in storage," she said. "I only brought jeans and casual tops. I don't have anything the least bit fancy, so going out to dinner isn't an option. Besides, if you feel like providing a meal in return, why don't you just pick up a pizza and bring it home one night?"

"I suppose I could do that."

She forced one of her best bright-eyed smiles, then focused on her plate, doing her best to ignore the romantic ambience she hadn't meant to set into motion.

Romantic ambience? Here on Granny's back porch?

Not that there was anything wrong with the cozy quarters, but there weren't any candles or flowers or music. The only thing remotely romantic was the thudding beat of Juliana's heart.

And the lingering memory of a heated kiss she wasn't likely to ever forget.

After they'd washed and put away the dinner dishes, something Jason again helped Juliana do, he asked if she'd like to return to the porch for coffee, a glass of wine, juice or…whatever.

"I'd like to," she said, "but I didn't get much sleep last night, so I want to turn in early. And since I have a doctor's appointment in town tomorrow afternoon,

I'm going to set my alarm clock so I can make up those hours first thing in the morning. I hope to get started on packing the hutch in the dining room—unless you'd rather I started somewhere else."

"No, that's fine." He wondered if she was only making an excuse to put some distance between them and their obvious attraction, but he decided it was best to let it drop. He needed her help with the inventory. He also knew better than to get romantically involved with an employee. His father had made that mistake once, only to be slapped with a charge of sexual harassment. The lawsuit had resulted in a lengthy litigation and a large settlement, a mistake Jason had no intention of repeating. But then again, his old man had probably been guilty as charged, and this situation seemed completely different.

Trouble was, now that Jason had kissed Juliana, he didn't know what to do about it. He'd have to do something, though. A man didn't just ignore a smoking-hot kiss with a beautiful redhead and write it off as if it hadn't happened.

Besides, ignoring the whole thing had damn near killed him during dinner, especially when her rosy cheeks let him know she'd been thinking about it, too.

Still, as Juliana left the kitchen and headed to her room, it was way too early for Jason to turn in. He didn't feel like watching television or holing up in the den, just steps away from where she'd be lying in bed. So he walked through the living room and headed out to the front porch, where the stars sparkled overhead and a somber country-and-western tune filled the night air.

He made his way to the wooden railing and peered at the small guesthouse, where the sole ranch hand, Ian McAllister, sat outside in one of two chairs, his guitar in his lap, his fingers strumming the strings.

Years ago, Reuben Montoya had been the foreman on the Leaning R and had done a fine job of running things. Then about five years ago, there'd been a family emergency, and Reuben had had to return to his hometown, a small village located somewhere near the coast in Baja California. Granny had hired several different men to take his place, but she'd had to let each one go because they'd fallen short of the benchmark Reuben had set. Finally, she'd taken on Ian. From what she'd said several times, Ian had pleased her. "He's got an inborn skill at ranching," she'd said, "and a way with sick or injured critters that's pert near better than any vet I've ever seen."

But when Granny passed, the Leaning R ownership had transferred to Jason's father, who hadn't made any secret that the ranch wasn't a priority to him. He could have given Ian free rein to make a go of things, but for some reason, he'd refused to even consider it. In fact, he hadn't even allowed Ian to hire on any new hands whenever one of the men quit and went on to work for other spreads. And without any qualified cowboys to help him, Ian had been limited to what he could do alone.

Jason was surprised the man had stuck around this long. But then again, he was a cowboy. And those guys had an interesting code of honor, even the younger ones in their midthirties, like Ian.

If Jason were inclined to turn things completely around, he'd let Ian see what he could do with the place. But Granny had wanted at least one family member to live on the ranch and oversee things. And that wasn't likely to happen. Braden had his own place ten miles down the road, Carly was dead set on building a singing career to surpass that of her mother's and Jason wasn't about to set down roots in Brighton Valley. His corporations were based in Houston—and so was his life.

As Ian's haunting melody filled the summer night, Jason swore under his breath. It was too early and too nice of an evening for him and Ian to be outside by themselves, bogged down by melancholy thoughts or sad music. So he strode into the kitchen, grabbed a couple of longneck beers from the fridge and crossed the yard.

When he reached the patch of lawn in front of Ian's place, the music echoed to a slow stop, and the cowboy glanced up. "What's up, boss?"

"I thought you might like a beer and some company. If not, I can leave the drink and go on my way."

Ian tossed him a lopsided grin. "I rarely drink these days." Then he took the Corona and nodded at the empty chair beside him. "But singing makes me thirsty and lonely. So thanks. And have a seat."

Jason didn't normally come out looking for Ian after dark. Nor did he have time to make chitchat. When they did talk, it was to line Ian out for the day or to get his opinion about something to make the ranch more valuable to a buyer. But for the most part, there'd been so much going on at both Rayburn offices that Jason had let Ian continue to handle most of the daily ranch decisions on his own.

"I owe you an apology," Jason said. "Not only have I done very little to help you, but I haven't gotten around to hiring those extra men I promised."

"I can find a couple of hands. All you have to do is say the word."

Jason took a swig of his beer. "I'll make it a priority tomorrow, although I may not get to it until midmorning."

"No problem." Ian tilted his own bottle and took a drink.

But that didn't assuage Jason's guilt. The man had been shouldering a lot for the past year. Yet he hadn't complained.

"If you're going into town," Ian said, "I have a few supplies that need to be picked up at the feed store."

"Will do."

The two men sat like that for a while—like drinking buddies mellowing out after a hard day's work. Yet they weren't buddies. They weren't…anything.

In fact, Ian probably knew Braden a hell of a lot better than he knew Jason, since they were both locals and ranchers. They had a lot more in common.

Had Ian been making comparisons between the half brothers?

The fact that he might have—and that Jason might have come up short—didn't sit well. And while Jason hadn't actually planned to come out here and strike up a friendship or to quiz the guy, neither seemed to be bad ideas now.

"I hear my brother is in Mexico," Jason said.

"Is that right?"

Didn't Ian know where Braden had gone? Or was he trying to avoid an inquisition?

"I figure he's got a good reason," Jason added, just in case Ian thought he was being set up. "And that he'll clue me in when the time is right."

"He didn't mention anything to me," Ian said.

For some reason, Jason believed him.

So much for the theory that the two Brighton Valley men were tight.

Ian, who'd been balancing his guitar in his lap, set the instrument down. "How's your sister doing?"

"Carly? She has a singing gig in San Antonio, so she's pretty excited about that."

"Glad to hear it. Maybe this is her big chance."

Jason wondered how Ian knew Carly. But then again, his sister had come by to visit regularly while Granny was still alive. And she still dropped by to check on the place occasionally. Apparently, Ian did more talking to Carly than he did to Braden. But Braden was so damned tight-lipped, and Carly...well, she'd sure been a jabber box, at least when she was a kid.

A grin tugged at his lips. He remembered the day when she and Bird Legs had come in from the swimming hole. They'd been all whispers and giggles back then. Juliana sure had changed, hadn't she?

His thoughts drifted from the past back to the present. Damn. Who would have guessed that the gangly little girl would have grown up to be such a shapely beauty?

He glanced at the house, at the window of the room that had once been Granny's, and watched the light go out. So she really was going to hit the sack early.

Had she heard Ian playing the guitar? Would the music lull her to sleep? The tune had certainly had a mesmerizing effect. He wondered what the words were.

"That was a nice song you were playing earlier," Jason told the foreman. "I don't think I've ever heard it before. Not that I'm a country fan these days. Is it a new recording or one that's been out for a while?"

"Actually, I wrote it myself."

"No kidding?"

Ian shrugged. "It's just a cowboy lullaby to put the little dogies to sleep."

"I'm no expert, but it sounded good to me. You probably shouldn't waste your talent on a bunch of cows."

Ian didn't comment. He just lifted his longneck and took another drink.

Had Carly ever heard him play? If so, had she encouraged him to do something with his music? Not that it mattered. Ian obviously liked being a cowboy and was content to play for himself. And Carly wanted to be on a stage. They had different dreams, different life paths.

Jason glanced at the house, where the porch light cast an amber glow, while Granny's bedroom remained dark. His and Juliana's paths had merged temporarily, but they'd soon go in opposite directions, too, just as Ian's and Carly's had.

But they were together for the time being…

Jason avoided commitments and anything long-term. You certainly couldn't blame him for that. Hell, just look at his father's track record.

Of course, that didn't mean he was opposed to a one-on-one relationship as long as it remained mutually beneficial. And right now, Jason was between lovers.

So was Juliana.

He might have made it a point not to get involved with employees or business associates, but Juliana was only a temporary hire.

Would it be wrong to see what developed between them—for as long as it lasted?

Jason had planned to run into town before lunch, but as luck—and the home office—would have it, he didn't get a chance to leave until after two o'clock.

As he was heading out of the house, he didn't spot Juliana in either the living room or the kitchen. He suspected she was getting ready for her doctor's appointment, so he left without telling her goodbye.

Although he would have preferred to stick around and finish the last project he'd been working on, he'd promised Ian he would hire some help, and he didn't want to let him down. So he snatched his hat from the hook by the back door, grabbed the keys to the ranch pickup and took off.

His first stop was Lone Star Hay and Feed, which had once been owned by Del Grimwood. Apparently the man had retired a few years back and sold the business. So Jason introduced himself to the new owner, a middle-aged man named Paco Ramirez.

He'd just hit End on a business call that hadn't gone well when he spoke, so his words came out a little more abrupt than he'd meant them to. "My father was Charles Rayburn, and his grandmother, Rosabelle, owned the Leaning R. I'm in charge now, so I've been staying out there—temporarily."

Paco shifted his stance, then crossed his arms. "I thought the world of your great-grandmother, and I knew your father. I went to high school with him. I also know Braden and his mother's family well. But just so you know, I judge a man by his character—not his bloodlines."

Jason hadn't meant to come across as high-and-mighty, but before he could apologize and tell the man he'd had his mind on his other business issues, Paco added, "Your father may be highly respected in California and in the business world where he once ran, but his reputation in this neck of the woods wasn't much to shout about. But I won't hold that against you—just like I didn't hold it against your brother."

Had his father left that bad of an impression on the townspeople?

Jason always figured his father had considered Brighton Valley to be a Podunk town that he'd outgrown. But did it have more to do with the fact that he'd gotten Braden's mother pregnant while he'd been married to Jason's mom?

That must have been a scandal that tarnished his

reputation, although he'd never missed a child support payment, as far as Jason had been told.

"I'm sorry, Mr. Ramirez. I didn't mean to be rude or to give you the wrong impression. Rest assured, I'm not like my father."

"I'm glad to hear that," Paco said. "What can I do for you?"

"I'm looking for some temporary hands on the Leaning R. Do you know anyone who'd be interested?"

Paco stroked his chin. "Does Ian still work for you?"

"Yes, and I need to find help for him."

"In that case, my oldest boy is looking for a summer job. He's only seventeen, but he's strong, a good worker and knows cattle and horses."

"Great. When can he start?"

"Tomorrow morning, I suspect."

"I'll tell Ian to expect him. What's his name?"

"Jesse."

Jason lifted his hat and readjusted it on his head. "Do you mind if I post an ad on your bulletin board?"

"No, go ahead. I'll keep my ears open, too. Temporary help isn't always as easy to find as a permanent position. But just so you know, Jesse's friends are all football players. They're good kids—strong, too. And they're not afraid of hard work. They're probably your best bet."

"Thanks. You might be right about that. Maybe your son could round up his buddies and bring them out to the ranch. I'd really appreciate it, and I know Ian would, too." Jason reached into his hip pocket and pulled out the list Ian had given him. "I also need to pick up these things while I'm here."

Twenty minutes later, he'd paid Paco and loaded the last of the sacks and boxes into the back of the ranch pickup. Then he was on his way into town.

His next stop was Nettles Realty, a small office on the shady, tree-lined main drag. He pulled into an empty parking stall near the drugstore, then crossed the street and entered the bright red door of the only real estate agent in town.

Granny had been friends with Helen, Ralph's wife. She used to work with him, but she'd gotten sick about the time Granny died. She was better now, but from what Jason had heard, Helen remained at home these days and Ralph worked alone.

Ralph was close to eighty years old and probably should have retired a long time ago, but he often quipped that he was no quitter. He was still spry and sharp. He also knew the area better than anyone else.

Jason greeted the snowy-haired gentleman who sat at a big oak desk cluttered with files and stacks of paper with a handshake. "I'm Jason Rayburn, Ralph. We talked on the phone a couple of days ago."

"Good to see you, son." The old man got to his feet. "I'm glad to get the listing, although I'm sorry to see the Leaning R sold. That ranch has been in your family for years."

A pang of guilt twisted Jason's gut. Harold and Molly Rayburn, Granny's in-laws, had been newlyweds when they'd homesteaded the land. They'd raised a family there. At least, they'd tried to. Harold and two of their children had died of the Spanish influenza early in the twentieth century. Dave, the only surviving child, had inherited the Leaning R and married Granny.

But Jason shook off his discomfort and pressed on. "The place isn't ready to show any prospective buyers yet, but I hope to have it clean, emptied and close to presentable within the next two weeks."

"What are you going to do with the furniture?"

"I have a woman helping me inventory it. Whatever Braden and Carly don't want, I plan to sell."

"Some of those things are antiques," Ralph said. "They might actually make the house show better, so keep that in mind."

"All right." After thanking the real estate agent for his time, Jason left. As he stepped out onto the sidewalk, the hearty aroma of Italian sausage, tomatoes, basil and garlic taunted him, and he glanced to the right at Maestro's, the new restaurant he'd wanted to try. A man in black slacks and a white dress shirt was spreading white linen over the black wrought-iron patio tables in preparation for the diners who preferred to eat outdoors.

Before Jason could cross the street and head toward the space where he'd parked his truck, a woman exited a store to the right. He didn't pay her any mind, but he did catch a glimpse of the mannequin in the window display of the Mercantile, the only dress shop in this part of town. It modeled a sexy black dress that was both formfitting and sleek.

An idea struck, and a smile spread across his face.

Juliana had mentioned that she didn't have anything suitable to wear to an eatery like Maestro's. What if he bought the dress for her as a surprise? He could call it a bonus. And he'd tell her the dinner was in celebration of getting a price for the ranch and finding a listing agent.

He wasn't sure of her size, but his sister had mentioned once that she was a six. And they were about the same height and shape.

What the hell.

Ten minutes later, a sales clerk who knew Carly and believed Jason was making the purchase for her had rung up the dress and placed it in a plastic bag with the Mercantile logo. After draping it over his arm, he left the store. He probably should have taken it to the pickup, but instead, he carried it with him to Maestro's, where he made dinner reservations for next Saturday evening at seven o'clock.

And speaking of dinner, since Juliana had a doctor's appointment, cooking wouldn't be on her to-do list today. So Jason would just stop by Caroline's Diner and pick up something to take home.

Rather than head to his truck first, he decided to place the order and then put away the dress while he was waiting for the food to cook.

It seemed simple enough, especially since Caroline's was just another couple of doors down from the Mercantile. Once inside the diner, he figured he'd make it quick by ordering the daily special, which Caroline displayed on a chalkboard near the register at the door. She always listed the offering as "What the Sheriff

Ate." Today it read: fried chicken, mashed potatoes and gravy, sweet corn and peach cobbler à la mode.

Jason placed the order with a middle-aged brunette waitress whose name tag read Margie.

"I know the special offers mashed potatoes," Margie said, "but you can have French fries if you'd rather."

He gave it some thought before asking, "What do you suggest?"

Margie leaned against the counter and grinned, clearly happy to offer her opinion. "Most folks prefer the mashed potatoes. It's a house specialty since Caroline always makes her gravy from scratch. But I wanted to let you know there was an option."

He tossed her a smile. "I'll go with the local preference."

"You won't be sorry. And how 'bout I just send the peach cobbler for dessert? I don't think the ice cream will travel too well. But if you have any back at the ranch, it'll be a nice finishing touch."

"When I used to come here as a kid, I always chose the German chocolate cake. I don't suppose Caroline has any of that today."

"You're in luck. We've got a couple of slices left." Margie jotted down his order. "It shouldn't take too long to get this ready. Why don't you have a seat?"

The door swung open before Jason had a chance to acknowledge Margie's words or tell her he'd be back in a few minutes. He glanced over his shoulder as Juliana walked in, her hair long and glossy, the curls dancing over her shoulders.

He didn't know who was more surprised to see the

other, but it was all he could do to hide the logo on the plastic bag that announced he'd been shopping at the ladies' store down the street.

Juliana had just left the doctor's office and stopped by the diner to pick up her last paycheck. But when she spotted Jason, her breath caught and her knees nearly buckled.

She'd known he'd gone to town, but she hadn't expected to run into him at Caroline's.

"Hey," he said, all decked out in cowboy casual, his thumbs tucked into the front pockets of his jeans. "It looks like you had the same idea I did."

"What was that?"

"To pick up dinner to take home. But I beat you to it." He smiled, which sent her heart skittering through her chest like a cat chasing its own tail. "How did your doctor's appointment go?"

"Doctor's appointment?" Margie asked. "You were just at the doctor a while back, Juliana. It couldn't have been two or three weeks ago. Is something wrong?"

A response wadded up in Juliana's throat.

Jason glanced at her, then at Margie. The poor guy had no idea that the sweet but gossipy waitress, like a Brighton Valley Lois Lane, had been listening to their conversation. And that she was ready to take note of every single word she'd heard and add her own spin to it.

But Juliana knew she'd better steer the subject in a safer direction before Margie began connecting dots and spreading her assumptions.

"My last visit to the clinic was a month ago, Margie. And this was just a recheck. Everything's fine."

Margie cocked her head, and her grip on the pencil seemed to raise and tighten. "What was the doctor rechecking?"

"It was…uh…sinus infection. All clear now." Juliana flushed and lowered her eyes. Doggone it. She considered honesty a virtue even more than most people, but now she had to add liar to her sinful résumé.

She placed her hand on her tummy, which she realized only served to draw attention to the growing bump. Then she let her fingers trail to her side and down along her thigh. As she did so, she stole a peek at Jason, wondering if he'd heard the deceit in her voice or spotted the guilty flush on her cheeks.

Instead, he seemed to be fiddling with the plastic shopping bag he'd rolled around his arm. Was he hiding something of his own?

Guilt was a funny thing, wasn't it? It seemed to make one suspicious of others.

"Well," she said. "There isn't any reason for us both to hang around and wait for the food. I think I'd better head back to the ranch. I got so much work done earlier today that I don't want to lose my momentum."

Nor did she want to stick around in Brighton Valley until Margie and everyone else in town uncovered the secret she was trying so hard to hide.

Chapter Five

Juliana continued to inventory the household items for the next several days. Jason helped when he could, but he spent the mornings in the office dealing with issues having to do with either Rayburn Energy or Enterprises.

Quite frankly, it was difficult for her to keep the two entities separate—especially when she wasn't privy to any of his telephone conversations and he rarely confided in her, anyway. At least, he hadn't since that first night when she'd made some suggested changes to the artwork his marketing department had been considering.

After eating a sandwich for lunch, he often went out onto the ranch to help Ian and several teenagers who'd come to work repairing the barn, the corrals and one of the outbuildings. The Ramirez boy and his friends were doing a good job. Both Ian and Jason seemed pleased with them.

In the evenings, Juliana cooked dinner, which Jason appreciated. At least, he complimented her on her efforts and asked for seconds. He also invited her to join him on the porch afterward. But ever since that heated kiss, she'd found one excuse or another to avoid being alone with him.

The only problem was, she was getting tired of going to her bedroom early each night and looking— and feeling—like a hermit. After all, sparks aside, she did enjoy his company. Maybe she could just…ignore those feelings in favor of some good old-fashioned conversation by starlight.

So tonight, after dinner, when he asked if she'd like to go out onto the porch, she finally agreed.

It must have surprised him because he broke into a smile. "That's great. But before we do, I have something I want to give you."

Now it was her turn to be surprised. "What is it?"

"Wait here."

When he disappeared through the doorway into the main part of the house, she pulled out a kitchen chair and took a seat at the antique oak table.

He returned before she knew it with a long plastic bag covering what had to be an article of clothing, because it hung from a coat hanger. It also had to be the same thing he'd been carrying when she'd run into him at Caroline's Diner.

"What's that?" she asked.

"A bonus for all the hard work you've done."

Her head tilted slightly to the side. "I don't understand."

He handed it to her. "Take it out."

She reached for the hanger and noted the Mercantile logo. He'd apparently purchased something for her, and she had no idea how to respond. But she probably ought to look inside before saying anything. So she removed the plastic, revealing a stylish black cocktail dress, a slinky, formfitting number that would have looked amazing if she still had a waistline. But there was no way it would possibly fit now. And even if it would, she couldn't accept it.

"I talked to Ralph Nettles about my plan to sell the ranch," he said, "and even though it isn't officially listed yet, I want to celebrate by going out to dinner tomorrow night—at Maestro's."

The gift and the invitation to help him celebrate jumbled her thoughts and robbed her of speech.

"Since you didn't have anything suitable to wear," he added, "I picked this up for you. Consider it a bonus for a job well done."

Was he serious?

A sweet but cocky grin suggested he was. And while his motives might be genuine and sincere, they reeked of those of the once-charming Alex Montgomery, the art dealer who'd swept into the gallery one day, set his sights on her, promising her the moon, then left her holding a handful of lies.

"I'm sorry." She passed the dress back to him. "I can't accept this. And I won't go out to dinner with you, either. I don't feel right about socializing with a coworker or an employer."

His grin faded, and an expression of remorse took its place. "I'm the one who's sorry. I didn't mean to offend you—or to come on too strong. I find you attractive, Juliana, and I wanted to spend some time with you away from work, away from the ranch. I'd like to get to know you better. But I don't want you to feel awkward or uncomfortable about it."

She bit down on her bottom lip, believing the first person to learn her secret should be her mother, but wondering if her new boss deserved a better explanation than the response she'd just given him.

"It's not what you're thinking," she said. "There's more to it than that."

A boyish grin, this one more confident than cocky, slid back into place. "You mean I didn't offend you or come on too strong?"

"No, I'm…flattered."

His smile deepened, and he moved forward.

She lifted her right hand to slow him down—or rather, to fend him off. "I'm pregnant."

He took a step back, as if she might be contagious, and she nearly laughed. In fact, she might have if a flood of tears hadn't filled her eyes to overflowing.

"Oh, jeez, Juliana. I'm sorry. Now I'm the one who feels awkward."

She might have let the chuckles flow, hoping to get some control over the emotions that had been bubbling inside her for the past four and a half months. But there really wasn't anything funny about it—other than the adorable look of utter embarrassment on the gorgeous CEO's face.

"Besides my doctor, you're the first in town to learn the news. I plan to tell my mother next, although the fact that I'm not married to the baby's father and will be raising my child on my own is sure to crush any excitement about being a new grandma. She has pretty high moral standards, and my situation will be sure to scandalize her if and when it gets out. I was hoping to tell her, then leave town. If we keep it a secret and I return a few years down the road, I can create a make-believe story to explain the baby by then."

"So that's why you plan to leave Brighton Valley so soon."

"You heard Margie at Caroline's Diner quizzing me a couple of days ago." She placed her hand on her growing womb, stroking the rounded slope. "As you can see, if I want to keep this a secret, my time in Brighton Valley is nearly up."

"Who's the father?"

"An art dealer who recently purchased stock in the gallery I worked in."

"Does he know about the baby?"

She paused for a moment, wondering just how much she cared to reveal. She was still reeling from the fact that the man she'd thought she loved had been living two different lives—one as a married father of three and the other as a footloose womanizer.

But that would mean she couldn't read people very well and that she'd been completely taken in by a lying jerk. And she hated to admit that her judgment was so poor.

"I made a big mistake by getting involved with the wrong guy," she admitted. "He wasn't the man he claimed to be. He knows about the baby, but he's not interested. In fact, he wanted me to 'get rid of it' and referred to it as a rug rat. But I refused. So for that and several other reasons, he'll never be a part of my life or my baby's."

"What about child support?" Jason asked.

"I'm going it alone. But don't worry. I'll be fine." And she would be.

She swiped a hand across her eyes. Her words might project confidence, but unfortunately, her over-productive tear ducts might not be as convincing.

Jason was stunned. He hadn't expected Juliana to turn him down—or to give him such a compelling reason. He should thank his lucky stars that he had the perfect excuse to run—and not walk!—away from all of that. Yet his...what, his heart? His conscience? Whatever it was seemed to hold him back and wouldn't let him hightail it too far away just yet.

His father had been a womanizer and had left Braden's mother in a similar situation. And while he might not have gotten other single women pregnant, he'd surely hurt them or made them feel as though he cared less for them than he'd first led them to believe.

And now, those women had a face. A lovely one, with flushed, tear-stained cheeks.

"What will you do to support yourself?" he asked.

"I'll find a job. In the meantime, I have this." Juliana swept her arm in front of her, indicating the work he'd given her at the ranch. "I also dabble in art and left a few pieces back at La Galleria in Wexler on consignment. Hopefully, they'll sell. Loren, the original owner, is going to forward the money to my mother. And she'll pass it on to me."

"So you're an artist," he said.

She gave him a halfhearted shrug. "I'd planned to be. Someday. But going on to a four-year university didn't work out. And now I'll be looking for employment I can depend on to support me and a baby."

He felt the urge to offer her a position at Rayburn Energy, but bit back what could only be considered an overzealous attempt to right his father's wrongs. All he needed was to have Juliana within arm's distance day in and day out. Or for her to feel beholden to him in some way. That would really muddle things at the office.

She slipped the dress back into the plastic bag and handed it to him. "Thanks for thinking of me. I certainly appreciate your generosity. But now you can see why I can't accept it."

"Keep it anyway. I'm sure you'll be able to wear it someday."

Her smile didn't reach her eyes, which glistened with tears that he feared could overflow again at any moment. "After the baby gets here, I doubt that I'll have an opportunity to go anywhere for quite a while, let alone to a place where I can wear something this nice."

The truth of her words filled the air, and so did

the unfairness of her situation. She'd be financially strapped and carrying the responsibility of her love child alone. And she was too young, too pretty, too...

He studied her a moment, caught up in... Hell, he had no idea what was swirling around him. It seemed to be the same attraction he'd felt earlier, but it couldn't be.

Was it respect, then? It had to be. That and maybe something more.

"That guy," he said, "the baby's father. He was a fool."

Her smile brightened. "Thanks. My ego needed to hear that."

Unable to help himself, he ran his knuckles along her cheek, and their gazes locked. Then, as if he'd lost all shred of good sense, he brushed a kiss across her lips.

Just to show his friendship, he told himself. His support.

But his arms seemed to have a rebellious mind of their own as they stole around her waist and drew her close. The kiss deepened, promising to light up the room in a burst of heat, just like before, but Juliana ended it almost as quickly as it began.

"I'm sorry," she said. "This isn't going to work."

"I know. I'm the one who should be sorry. I didn't mean for that to happen. It just did, and it was out of line."

Out of line? He'd been out of his mind, too. What had provoked him to kiss her again? She'd given him the perfect opportunity to cut bait and to get back on an even keel.

She placed her hand, the fingers splayed, at the base of her throat and took a step back. "I think it's best if you find someone else to finish up the inventory. I'll help out until my replacement arrives."

She was right, of course. But what was he going to do if she quit?

His gut clenched at the thought of her leaving. How odd that he'd feel that way about losing an employee who could be replaced.

Especially one who was expecting another man's baby.

Jason slept like hell that night and woke early the next morning. Rather than face Juliana and discuss the inappropriate kiss that had probably ruined a successful working arrangement, he fixed a cup of coffee, went into the den and began his day by checking email and catching up on the issues going on at the Houston office.

One of the first messages he received was from Doug Broderick, his right-hand man.

Jason,
I've attached the graphics with your suggested changes to the art layout. Craig, the marketing director, was impressed and thinks you're really onto something. I agree. What do you think of it now?
Doug

Jason studied the revised graphics, realizing Juliana's suggestions had made a big difference and provided that spark the artwork had been missing.

How about that? he mused.

Should he mention to Doug where the idea had come from? It wasn't as though he wanted to steal the credit for himself, but how deep did he want to get involved with Juliana?

Craig had suggested a shake-up in the marketing department to get some new blood. What if he wanted to interview the woman who'd taken one glimpse at the art layout and solved their dilemma within seconds with a simple suggestion?

Juliana needed a job, but she'd already told him she thought it was best that he find someone else to work for him. He couldn't very well sing her praises to the art department then. And that wasn't the only reason.

Granted, she had an innate talent and would be a great addition to an art department someday. But according to Carly, Juliana had never finished college. And she herself admitted that she only dabbled in art. So she wasn't entirely qualified for the position with his company at this particular time.

On top of that, there was the personal dilemma that was impossible to ignore. With the obvious chemistry they had—and the passion that was ready to ignite every time he got within arm's length of her—he couldn't very well risk passing her in the hall or bumping into her on the elevator, now could he?

Still, he wasn't about to use her suggestion without offering her any compensation. He knew the struggle she'd be facing over the next months—and possibly years.

Hell, maybe he could tell her that he'd set up a scholarship foundation for single mothers intending to finish their education. And that he was giving one to her.

Now there was an idea. He could call it the Charles Rayburn Love 'Em and Leave 'Em Foundation, created in an effort to make things right for jilted women around the world. And he could provide the first scholarship to Juliana.

Jason blew out a ragged sigh. Actually, all kidding aside, that wasn't entirely out of the question. He'd have to give it some thought. In the meantime, he had an email to answer.

Doug,
It looks great. I thought that would work. Tell Craig to run with it and see what his crew can come up with now.
Jason

He felt a momentary twang of guilt for taking any credit at all for her idea, but he hit Send anyway. If he hadn't seen the merit, he wouldn't have suggested it to Doug in the first place. Besides, he was going to lose Juliana anyway. Hadn't she told him last night that she'd be leaving?

That reminded him. He'd need to find a replacement—even if he doubted he could find anyone who'd come close to filling her shoes.

He'd no more than moved on to the next project on his to-do list when her voice sounded in the doorway.

"Excuse me," she said, "I hate to bother you, Jason, but I found something you need to see."

He glanced up from the file on his desk and spotted a black leather briefcase in her hand. His father's? It sure looked like it. "Where'd you find that?"

She entered the den and made her way to the front of his desk. "In one of the guest rooms. It was sitting up next to a wing-back chair. I looked inside to see if I could tell who it belonged to, and I found some files and papers that must be your father's. So I thought you'd better go through it instead of me."

That meant his dad had stopped by the ranch recently—before going to Mexico three months ago. Why had he done that?

Had Ian seen him? If so, Ian hadn't mentioned it. But then, Jason hadn't asked. He'd had no reason to believe his dad would have come here.

Jason opened the briefcase, but it didn't take long to realize what Juliana had pieced together. The briefcase had, indeed, belonged to Charles Rayburn. He'd either left it here on purpose, intending to return, or he'd forgotten it.

"Did you find anything else in that room?" he asked. "Any clothes or toiletries?"

"I haven't gone through the closets or the bathroom yet. But I'll go and look now."

"Thanks. I'd appreciate that."

And he would. He was overwhelmed with chores to do around here, both inside and out. And while he'd let Ian do most of the ranch work, and Juliana handled things in the house, that reminded him. How was he going to get everything done if Juliana left?

Braden was still in Mexico, and if Carly's show was a hit, who knew when either of them would step up to relieve him or help out. He could hire someone to replace Juliana, but they'd created such a comfortable working relationship—at least, when he wasn't tempted to kiss her.

After Juliana returned to the guest room where she'd been working, Jason sorted through the briefcase, releasing the spicy scent of his father's aftershave, as well as a hint of the peppermint breath mints he'd favored.

For a moment, Jason felt like a boy again, stealing a peek into his father's domain, hoping for a minute or two of the man's time. But his father was gone. As usual. This time permanently.

As he read over the files, he realized they were all recent. Most of them needed to be back at Rayburn Enterprises. He probably should ship them overnight.

Footsteps sounded in the hallway as Juliana returned. "The closet was empty. So was the bathroom. It looks like the briefcase was all he left."

She leaned against the doorjamb, her hair a tumble of red curls. For a moment, he forgot about his father, his work, his responsibilities to the trust or his siblings. Instead, he studied the lovely young woman who'd crossed his path and momentarily upended his world.

Her baby bump, if you could call it that, barely showed through the blousy green top she wore. Yet it gave her an intriguing appeal—the kind a man could come home to.

But he quickly shook it off. "I'm going to have to send the paperwork back to the office. Do you know where I can find the nearest FedEx or UPS place?"

"The only one I'm aware of is in Wexler, a couple of doors down from the art gallery where I worked."

Jason suspected there was one in Brighton Valley, which would probably be closer, but rather than search on his iPhone, he decided to drive into Wexler. While he was there, he might even swing by La Galleria and check out the deadbeat dad who'd fathered her baby.

He had no idea why it mattered who the guy was and what he looked like, but for some crazy reason, it did.

Forty-five minutes later, Jason left the Wexler FedEx office. But before climbing into his pickup to return to the ranch, he walked a couple of doors down the street to La Galleria, the place where Juliana had worked.

He paused at the glass door for a moment, tamping down a last-minute reluctance to enter, then proceeded to walk in.

Two salesmen stood inside, ready to help an interested buyer. The one behind the register was short, balding and in his fifties. He didn't seem to be a likely baby daddy possibility.

The other was the right age—midthirties, dark hair and not bad-looking, if you liked flashy dressers. His pearly white smile suggested he'd had some expensive cosmetic dentistry.

"Good afternoon," Smiley said. "Let me know if I can be of any help."

"I'm just looking," Jason said as he browsed the artwork on display.

Juliana had mentioned that she had a couple of paintings on commission, so he bypassed the pottery and statues and focused on the art that hung on the walls instead. He had no idea whether he should be looking for oils or watercolors or a particular style, so he focused on the signatures instead.

Surprisingly, he found one. It was a cowboy riding the range. The man was in the distance and wore a black hat, so there weren't any facial features to discern. But the trees were well done, as was the bay gelding he rode and the meadow on the hillside.

It wouldn't go with the decor of his condominium or his office in the downtown high-rise, but Ralph the real estate agent had suggested he make the ranch appealing to buyers. The painting would look good over the mantel in the living room.

The price was five hundred dollars. He wondered how much of it Juliana would get. The bulk of it, he hoped.

"I like this one," he said.

Sensing a sale, Smiley slid up next to him. "Nice choice. The artist also has two other paintings here."

"I'd like to see them."

Smiley moved to the left and pointed to one of a swimming hole that looked a lot like the one in Brighton Valley. A blonde girl with pigtails sat high on a branch, where a rope had been tied. It had swung over the water, and there was a big splash on the surface of the pond, as if another child had dropped underwater.

Just like in the first painting, the face was turned away and too far in the distance to recognize. It had to be the old swimming hole, although he didn't remember so many wildflowers on the grass. Juliana must have added them for effect. It was a nice touch. The cowboy had been riding near a meadow, too. The fact that she appreciated flowers and color didn't surprise him.

"And this is the third piece she has displayed," Smiley added, pointing to a picture of an outhouse with a crescent moon carved on the door.

Now that was unusual, although what drew a smile to Jason's lips were the saddled Appaloosa and the Australian shepherd seated on its haunches, apparently waiting patiently for their master to finish his business inside the outhouse.

Jason wasn't an art aficionado, so he couldn't comment on the quality or on Juliana's skill. But he thought they were good—if you liked Western art.

"What do you know about this artist?" he asked.

"She has talent," Smiley said.

"Is she local?"

"Yes."

"How many of her pieces do you have?"

"Just three right now, although I can get more for you."

Don't bother, Jason nearly told him. *I don't need a middleman, especially you.*

A woman entered, and Smiley turned to her. "Hey, baby. I'll be with you in a few."

"That's all right. The kids and I can meet you at the hamburger place."

"You go on and have dinner with your family," the older man said. "I can lock up the gallery, Alex."

So, Smiley had a name. As well as a wife and kids. Was that what Juliana had meant when she'd said that her baby daddy wasn't the man he'd claimed to be?

Of course, Jason didn't know for sure that Smiling Alex was the guy who'd misled her and asked her to get rid of the baby.

"Thanks, Loren." Alex stepped away from Jason and made his way toward his family." You don't mind locking up for the night?"

"No. I'll take care of things. You go on. The kids are probably hungry."

"These rug rats are always hungry," he said, mussing the hair of the tallest boy.

Maybe he was the baby daddy after all. Either way, Jason still didn't care for him.

When Alex and his family left, Jason asked, "Do you work on commission?"

"Alex and I are co-owners," Loren said, "so it doesn't matter. And as for the artist you were asking about, she used to work here up until two months ago. I was sorry to lose her, but I suppose it was just as well. Once Alex purchased half the stock, he moved his family to Wexler, so we would have had to cut her hours anyway."

"So," Jason said, "I take it Alex isn't from around here."

"No, he was an art dealer who used to come to town regularly. But his wife got tired of all his traveling and asked him to settle down. He decided Wexler would be a good place to raise his kids and asked me if I'd like to sell half my stock in the gallery. I was thinking about retiring in the near future, so I agreed."

"When did his wife and kids move here?"

"Just a few weeks ago. Right before Juliana left. I'll sure miss that girl. She was like a daughter to me."

Who else could Alex be but Juliana's ex and the father of her baby? He was a real piece of work. He reminded Jason of his father. But Charles Rayburn had taken care of his kids—at least financially.

"I'll take all three of these paintings," Jason said.

Loren grinned. "Great. I'll ring them up."

The cost would be more than a thousand dollars, which was quite a bit to grace the walls of a ranch house Jason intended to sell. But he was determined to add to Juliana's coffers.

And to give her another reason not to step foot in La Galleria again.

Chapter Six

Perspiration gathered at Juliana's brow and neck, dampening her curls, so she left the list she'd been compiling in the dining room and headed to the bathroom to pull her hair into a ponytail. Then she proceeded to open the windows and turn on the fans, something she should have done much earlier in the day.

The muggy summer heat had filled the house until it was almost unbearable, and she was going to take a shower so she could cool off.

As she headed for the bathroom, the phone rang and she changed directions so she could answer. It was Jason.

"I hope you haven't started cooking anything for dinner," he said.

Apparently, it was her turn tonight. She glanced at

the antique clock on the mantel. It was already after five, but she hadn't even given it a thought. In fact, she wasn't going to do anything before cooling down and taking a rest. And there was no way she'd be getting near a stove or an oven. "Not yet, but don't expect anything fancy. I'm thinking a sandwich or a bowl of cereal is about all I have the energy for."

"Don't worry about it. I'm going to bring something home. Do you like Chinese food?"

"That sounds great."

"Good. I'll be there in about forty-five minutes."

When the line disconnected, she grabbed a towel from the linen closet, then took a long, refreshing shower. Afterward, she lay down and closed her eyes for a short catnap.

She'd no more than rolled out of bed and entered the living room when she realized she'd dozed longer than she'd planned. Jason had already returned. He stood near the hearth, unwrapping a painting.

"What's that?" she asked.

"I went shopping while I was in Wexler." As he cast aside the brown paper that had protected the artwork, he revealed the painting she'd done of Braden.

Not that Jason would recognize his brother's favorite horse—or any of the places where Juliana and Braden used to ride.

"What do you think?" He lifted the painting. "I need to sell everything in the house, but Ralph Nettles suggested I should have a few things here to attract the buyers. I thought some Western artwork on the walls might do the trick."

Juliana crossed her arms. "I don't understand."

His smile faltered. "I stopped by the art gallery while I was in Wexler."

"I can see that. But why?"

"I was just curious about the type of things they carried. And I liked this painting."

Apparently, since he'd paid the five-hundred-dollar price.

"I also knew you could use the sale," he added. "So it was a win-win for both of us."

Something didn't seem right. Juliana might have been gullible before Alex Montgomery waltzed into her life and spun his web of deceit, but she'd learned to be skeptical and wasn't about to accept a handsome man's explanation at face value anymore—especially if she had reason to believe he might have an ulterior motive.

Why had Jason gone into La Galleria? Was he snooping into her past? Was he trying to play on her vulnerabilities and buy her affections?

Staying here on the ranch, helping him out, wasn't working out the way she'd hoped. And while she needed the money, she couldn't risk getting caught up in another...what? Dead-end romance?

But what if she was making more out of it than it really was? What if he'd only been trying to help her out? She'd been overly trusting once. Was she too skeptical now?

He set the painting of Braden aside and reached for a smaller one he'd leaned against the brown recliner. "I picked up this one, too."

As he unwrapped his next purchase, she realized

he'd also chosen another piece she'd left on consignment at La Galleria—the one of her and Carly at the old
swimming hole. Well, it wasn't actually *her*. She would
be the child who'd splashed underwater. But the blonde
in pigtails on the branch was Jason's younger sister.

Didn't he realize that?

Maybe not. Her back and hair were the only things
that showed. Juliana didn't paint faces. At least not
when her subjects were people she knew.

"Is this the old swimming pond?" he asked.

She smiled and nodded. "I wondered if anyone in
Wexler would recognize it."

"Most kids around here would," he said. "But I don't
remember any wildflowers."

"There are usually a few scattered about, but I added
a lot more. I like color in my paintings."

"It's a nice touch. I thought the house could use a
little pick-me-up, too, especially when Granny's things
are gone."

So he was determined to resell her paintings along
with the house. She supposed it didn't matter that he
didn't plan to keep them for himself. After all, she
would receive her commission. But part of knowing
that her art had sold was believing the buyer had liked
them enough to place them somewhere special, to sense
the love she'd felt when she'd created them.

As Jason tore into the brown-paper wrapping of the
third frame, she knew what he would uncover—the last
remaining painting she'd left at La Galleria—the one
of the old-style outhouse in a meadow.

Ironically, all the paintings were linked to the

Rayburn family. Not that she'd done it on purpose. It's just that her family ranch was gone, so she'd used the backdrops that were most familiar to her—Granny's ranch and Braden's.

The meadow where Braden rode his bay gelding was where she'd sometimes ridden with him, while the swimming hole was where Braden used to take her and Carly to swim.

And the outhouse?

That was the wildest connection of all—and really, just a figment of Juliana's imagination. Granny had once told her and Carly that Harold Rayburn, her father-in-law, used to have an Appaloosa mare and a cattle dog that followed him everywhere he went. *Why, folks said the poor man couldn't even go to the outhouse by himself*, Rosabelle had said. *Those critters would wait outside till he came out.*

The memory had just stuck, she supposed.

So while Jason was ridding the house of family memories, he was unknowingly replacing them with other Rayburn images on the walls.

Did she dare mention that to him?

In spite of what he planned to do with the Leaning R, it seemed as if the Rayburn family was destined to maintain some kind of claim on it anyway.

Jason had no more than opened the first takeout carton when Juliana swept into the kitchen like a cool summer breeze.

"I was just thinking," she said, "it's awfully warm in here. Why don't we eat outside tonight?"

"Good idea. Let's use paper plates, so there won't be any cleanup. And if you're comfortable with chopsticks, we won't even have to wash silverware."

Juliana tossed him a pretty smile. "Chinese food doesn't taste nearly as good if you eat it with a fork."

He studied her for a moment. She'd been wearing jeans when he'd left for Wexler. And now, in bare feet and a yellow sundress, she looked as fresh as the proverbial daisy. Or maybe a field of wildflowers. She smelled like it, too. Something floral. Jasmine, maybe?

"I don't blame you for showering," he said. "If I weren't so hungry and didn't want the food to get cold, I'd take one, too."

"I couldn't help it. I was busy and forgot to open up the windows. It got so warm and stuffy in here, I thought I'd melt."

In the summer, the old house could get hotter than blazes some afternoons if you didn't open things up and get the fans going early. Thank goodness Granny's room had a swamp cooler in the window.

Jason wondered if he should talk to Ralph about putting in an air-conditioning unit. Would that make the property any more appealing to a buyer? That was the first thing he'd want to add to the place, along with updating the kitchen and bathrooms. But then again, some people might like the authentic appeal of an old-style ranch house.

"I saw some citronella candles in the mudroom yesterday," Juliana added. "Maybe I should set them out on the porch to keep the bugs away."

"I'll set the table while you're fighting off the mosquitoes."

Five minutes later, they were seated outside, chopsticks in hand. The flames of four candles lined the wooden railing, flickering to fend off any winged insects out for blood. Yet it added an unintended romantic aura, too. And to make matters worse—or rather, nicer, depending upon how you looked at it—Ian chose that moment to sit on his own porch and strum his guitar, serenading them with a country love song.

"I didn't know Ian was a musician," she said. "Or that he could sing."

"He plays to relax sometimes."

"He's very talented."

Jason thought so, too, but he wasn't sure he should comment for fear it would make it sound as if he'd planned a romantic dinner under the stars. Of course, Juliana was the one who'd suggested eating outside.

A slight breeze kicked up, cooling the air and making the night even more pleasant. Yet as hungry as he was, he couldn't help but gaze at Juliana.

She was dressed casually this evening and had pulled her hair, a mess of damp red curls, into a ponytail that rode high on her head. She wasn't wearing any makeup, but she didn't need any props to draw a man's eye. She had a natural beauty that must have blossomed sometime during her teen years. He wished he could have been around to see the transformation. It must have been something to watch unfold.

In the candlelight, she seemed prettier than ever.

It was going to be tough to keep his hands—and his lips—to himself.

As she dug into the helping of chicken chow mein on her plate with a pair of chopsticks, she said, "Mmm. This is really good. Did you pick it up at Chin's Dynasty in Wexler?"

"That's the place." Her former boss, the man who'd rung up the sale for Smiling Alex, had suggested it.

Jason hadn't planned to talk to her about the gallery or about the men who worked there. Yet now that the subject had come up, he couldn't stop the niggle of curiosity from building until it urged him to say, "I met the newest owner of La Galleria."

Her movements stilled, the empty chopsticks dangling between her fingers as though they might fall onto her plate.

"Did you know he was married?" Jason asked.

"Of course not!" Shock and anger splashed across her face, yet he'd bet his question had hurt her, too.

In the background, Ian played another song about love that would last forever and ever. But there wasn't anything romantic, sweet or eternal about the conversation Jason had just broached.

He wished he could reel the question back. It really wasn't any of his business. Yet for some crazy reason, he wanted to know the details—needed to know them.

Juliana lay down her chopsticks, picked up her napkin and blotted her lips. "I told you he wasn't the man he led me to believe he was. If I'd known he was married or in a committed relationship I wouldn't have given him the time of day. But I thought I was the only woman he was seeing, the only woman he cared about. I didn't even know he had *children*."

"I'm sorry," Jason said. And he was. He might not make long-term commitments, but he never lied to the women he dated or made promises he couldn't keep.

A few moments passed, yet Juliana hadn't commented on his apology—nor had she picked up her chopsticks again.

"Do you still love him?" he asked.

"No. I loved the man I thought he was, but not the jerk he turned out to be. And once I learned the truth about him, I quit my job and left town."

"So you leaving your job had nothing to do with his family moving to Wexler?"

The look she shot him could have humbled a lesser man.

Hell, it humbled him. "I'm sorry," he said again. "I didn't mean to question your ethics or to stir up old wounds. I was just…curious. And concerned."

"Don't be. I'm going to be just fine."

"I'm sure you will be." But that didn't mean he wouldn't like to punch the married baby daddy's lights out.

"I don't owe you or anyone an explanation, but I ended things when I told him about the baby and he wanted me to get rid of it."

By the way she caressed her tummy, by that dreamy look she'd get whenever he did, he could see why the guy's callous solution would upset her.

"When I told him I wanted to keep the baby, he decided to come clean about his wife and family. I guess he figured I'd realize how a pregnancy would complicate our lives. But it wasn't just a complication to me. His revelation made me nauseous, and I'd never suffered any morning sickness up to that point."

The whole thing knotted Jason's gut, too, and he pushed his plate aside.

"I was making plans to give my notice because Alex was an art dealer who frequented the gallery often, and I wanted to avoid him. But when he purchased half the shop and moved his family to town, I hurried the process."

"Does your boss know any of this?"

"Fortunately, Alex had always insisted upon keeping our relationship quiet, although I thought it was because he was a private person—not because he didn't want my boss to find out about us. Hopefully, no one knows how foolish I was to get involved with him in the first place."

Jason could understand her embarrassment. He reached for a fortune cookie and handed it to her. "I have a feeling things are going to be looking up for you from here on out."

"I hope so. Things couldn't get much worse than they were two months ago." She tore into the cellophane, cracked open her cookie, read her fortune and laughed.

"What's it say?"

"'The right choice isn't always easy, but when you make it, your heart's dream will come true.'"

"See? What did I tell you?"

"Okay, smarty-pants." She handed him the remaining cookie. "What does yours say?"

After reading his, he slowly shook his head. "You can't believe this."

"What is it?"

"It's the same as yours."

"No way." She reached for his cookie. When she read his fortune, her jaw dropped. "That never happens."

"Are we supposed to pinky swear or something?" he asked.

She laughed. "That's too weird. I guess we can blame it on the cookies being mass-produced in a factory."

"Or fortunes being mass-printed, I guess." As Jason packed up the carton of sweet-and-sour pork, the house phone rang.

"I'll get it," Juliana said. "I was going to take the dirty plates and napkins to the kitchen anyway."

She answered on the third ring. "Hello?" She paused. "Braden, is that you? I'm sorry, there's a lot of static on the line."

The minute Jason heard his brother's name he got to his feet and headed into the house. Juliana hadn't confirmed it was Braden or not, but on the outside chance that it was, he wanted to talk to him.

"I'm here because I'm helping Jason with the inventory," she said, pausing again, apparently listening to the voice on the other line. "I know. And I will. Let me get your brother." Juliana handed him the receiver. "It's Braden. But there's a bad connection."

Without bothering to say hello, Jason asked, "What's going on?"

"I should ask you that," Braden said. "What's Juliana doing there?"

"Carly had to go to San Antonio for a singing job, and she suggested that Juliana help me at the ranch."

"Yeah, well, watch your step with her. She's a good girl from a decent family."

Jason bristled. "What do you mean by that?"

"Nothing, except she's not your usual type. So I hope you won't take advantage of her."

"I don't intend to." Did Braden know about Juliana's pregnancy? She'd said no one else did, but he sounded so protective. Maybe he knew about her breakup.

If so, was he staking some kind of claim on her?

Jason didn't like thinking that he was. Nor did he like the sense of jealousy that shimmied over him.

The telephone line crackled, and before he lost the connection, he had a few questions for his brother. "Why are you in Mexico? And what's the deal with Dad hiring a private investigator?"

"He was looking for Camilla Cruz," Braden said. "And I'm following up on that."

Before Jason could quiz his brother further, the line buzzed, then went dead. "Dammit." He hung up the phone and turned to Juliana. "Did Braden ever mention Camilla Cruz?"

"The woman who painted Granny's portrait? No, why?"

"Braden is in Mexico looking for her. Apparently,

my father was doing the same thing. The connection was so bad, I didn't get a chance to ask anything else."

"Why don't you do an internet search on the woman and see if you can learn more about her?"

"Good idea."

Leaving the food and the flickering candles on the porch, they went into the den. Jason's laptop was only hibernating, so they didn't have to wait long to run the search.

Juliana stood at his side, her scent snaking around him and reminding him they'd become a team of sorts. At least, they had while working at the house.

He'd yet to come clean about the helpful suggestions she'd given him for that art layout, though. Again, he told himself that was for the best. They had different futures mapped out for themselves, in spite of what the fortune cookies might have implied.

Besides, she was pregnant. And Jason wasn't cut out to be a family man.

As the search engine screen opened up he typed, "Camilla Cruz, Artist" into the search line, then waited to see what popped up. Her website hadn't been updated in two years, but there was a bio page.

Camilla Cruz, a thirty-six-year-old artist, was born in San Antonio and showed talent at an early age. Her father worked on a cattle ranch in Texas and poured his life savings into art classes for her. She later opened galleries in Guadalajara and Mexico City, but had sold them recently and retired.

At thirty-six? That was odd.

After checking a few other sites, the only new bit

of information they picked up was that she had died of breast cancer in San Diego last year.

"It seems a simple internet search could have given my dad and Braden the answers they needed," Jason said.

"Maybe it merely provided them with more questions."

Juliana was probably right. Why had the woman been so important? If Granny were alive, he'd ask her. She would have known the answer. As it was, he was in the dark until he could get through to Braden again.

On a whim, he reached for his iPhone and dialed his brother's cell. But it only rang through. He must be in some remote location. Where had Braden's search taken him? And what else had he learned about Camilla Cruz and their father's interest in the woman that he hadn't been able to share before the line disconnected earlier?

"Braden's obviously not in one of the bigger Mexican cities," Juliana said.

"Did he say anything else to you?" Jason asked. "Before you handed me the receiver?"

Actually, he had. But Juliana didn't think Jason would appreciate knowing Braden's exact words. *Be careful of my brother. He's too much like my father.*

"You mean about Camilla?" she asked.

Jason studied her for a moment, as if he knew she was holding something back. "Did he say anything at all?"

She gave a little shrug. "Not really. He didn't want you to take advantage of me, that's all."

Jason stiffened. "I wouldn't do that."

"I guess Braden isn't so sure."

Probably not. Braden didn't know much about Jason. But then, how could he? They'd never spent much time together. And even when they had, they'd kept each other at arm's distance.

"Are you and Braden close?" he asked.

Juliana wasn't sure what he meant by that. "We're good friends. Neither of us had brothers or sisters…" She paused, realizing her mistake. "Well, he didn't have any living in his house. So we leaned on each other in some ways. You know what I mean?"

"I'm afraid not. I didn't lean on either my brother or my sister."

"That's too bad. You missed out. Carly's a lot of fun and a very supportive friend. And Braden's…" She let it go. Apparently, there was bad blood between them, and she wasn't sure she should get involved in trying to mend that. She wouldn't be around long enough.

Jason glanced down at the desk, although she suspected he was looking right through the files and papers he'd left in piles there.

Was he thinking about the relationships he had with his siblings? Did he wish they got along better? Or was he okay with things the way they were?

If so, it was his loss. She'd meant what she said about Carly and Braden.

For a moment, Jason looked a bit like a lost little boy, a child who'd had everything taken away from him. Yet that couldn't possibly be true. He'd grown up in the lap of luxury and had everything money could buy.

Or was that the problem? Did he realize the best things in life couldn't be purchased?

She wanted to tell him everything would be okay, but how could she possibly promise him a thing like that when she was doing her best to convince herself of that very thing?

Yet her hormones—and not just the new maternal ones that were pumping inside her—were nearly overwhelming, urging her to reach out, to touch him.

She placed her hand on his shoulder, felt the heat of his body, the strength of him. When he looked up and caught her eye, something sparked between them, connecting them in a way that went beyond words, beyond touch.

He must have felt it, too, because he reached up and covered her hand with his, melding her to him. It was both exhilarating and unnerving at the same time, and her heart scampered in her chest like a frightened puppy that didn't know if it should find a way out or a warm, cozy place and stay put.

Who was Jason Rayburn? Rigid, decisive CEO? Or a strong man who'd been wounded as a child?

Either way, she couldn't remain connected to him or to his ranch. She slid her hand out from under his and nodded toward the doorway. "We left the candles burning outside. I'm going to blow them out."

"I'll help."

"You don't need to."

As she padded down the hall, his footsteps sounded

behind her. Both Carly and Braden had told her that
Jason, like their father, was self-centered and unap-
proachable. But she had a feeling that wasn't true. Too
bad she couldn't stick around long enough to…

To do what? To learn more about the man behind
the myth? To fix things between the siblings? She was
afraid that would take more time than she had—as well
as a miracle. And she didn't have any of those up her
sleeve, either.

In the past week, she'd gotten a lot of items inven-
toried and packed away, but there was still a ton to do.
She hated to leave him high and dry, but there was no
way she could continue working for him under the
circumstances. He stirred her emotions, which were
far too vulnerable, thanks to her maternal hormones.
Okay, so her feminine ones were swirling around and
complicating things, too.

Not that she believed there was any truth to Braden's
warning. She really didn't think Jason would try to take
advantage of her. He seemed to be just as perplexed by
their attraction as she was. But she couldn't risk getting
involved with anyone right now. Her feelings were too
raw, and her future was up in the air.

As she blew out the candles on the porch railing,
Jason gathered up the leftovers, as well as the empty
cartons.

"I'm going to toss the fortunes," he said, "unless
you want to keep yours."

"Maybe I should keep them both to prove that
they're not as unique as people might think."

"And to remind you that you'll be getting your heart's wish, now that you decided to dump Smiley."

"Who?"

"Sorry. I made up a nickname for him. Well, a couple of them, actually. But that's the only one that's appropriate to say in mixed company."

She laughed. "I have a few names I've called him, too. But no, go ahead and throw away the fortunes. I don't need to keep them as a souvenir. I don't put any stock in that sort of thing."

"Neither do I. Besides, I try my best to make the right decisions every day."

"The fortune cookie was talking about *choices*. That's different."

"I can't see how."

"A decision is made with your brain. But a choice is made with your heart."

He gazed at her for a moment, his eyes zeroing in on hers and sending her pulse soaring. "I thought you majored in art, not linguistics or philosophy."

"Believe it or not, Braden's the one who taught me the difference."

"No kidding? How did he do that?"

"I told you there was a lot about your brother you didn't know."

"That's not news to me, Juliana. My brother and I are practically strangers."

"It doesn't have to be that way. You have a choice."

"So does he."

"But someone has to choose to make the first move." With that, Juliana tucked three candles in the crook of her left arm, grabbed the last one and headed into the house.

If there were anything mystical involved, it would seem that she and Jason had each received the proper fortune this evening. They both had critical choices to make—about what was right. And while he had yet to make his, she'd already made hers, which really hadn't been difficult at all. She'd chosen to keep the baby, to break up with Alex and to move to Houston.

Her heart's dream had always been to become an artist or to work with art somehow. But unfortunately, that wouldn't come true for a very long time.

Chapter Seven

On Saturday morning, Ralph Nettles stopped by the ranch to take a look at the property and give Jason his thoughts on an asking price.

"I haven't been inside since your grandmother's funeral," Mr. Nettles said as he eyed the stacks of boxes Juliana had packed and labeled after she'd carefully listed each item on the spreadsheet. "It's a shame you're not going to keep it in the family."

"My great-grandmother wanted one of us to live here and oversee the ranch, but my house and businesses are in Houston. My sister wants a singing career and is in San Antonio now, but she plans to travel. And Braden can't run two places at once."

"That's true." The white-haired man nodded slowly and stroked his chin. "Braden's granddad hasn't been well, and so your brother will be busier than ever, especially if Gerald passes."

Juliana knew that Gerald Miller had been under the weather, but she hadn't known that it was that serious.

"What's wrong with Mr. Miller?" Jason asked.

"Cancer. I've seen him a few times when I take my wife to see her oncologist. Gerald doesn't talk much, but he told her, at his age, he wasn't going to fight it. He didn't see the point. And I can't say as I blame him. That chemo can take a lot out of a man, especially if it isn't going to do the trick for very long."

Juliana wondered if Braden knew. If so, he hadn't said anything to her. And even though he was fairly private, she suspected he would have mentioned something. She also wondered if Mr. Miller would appreciate Mr. Nettles sharing the news of his illness or his thoughts on treatment with them.

She didn't think so.

"That's too bad," Jason said.

"Sure is. They don't make too many folks like the Millers. They're good people."

That was true. Juliana glanced at Jason, saw his brow furrow. Had Mr. Nettles's assessment surprised him?

"Why don't I show you the rest of the house," he suggested to the Realtor. "Then I'll take you out and give you a tour of the ranch."

"You aren't going to make me saddle up, are you?" Mr. Nettles chuckled. "I used to be a pretty good rider, but these days I'm a little rusty."

"Don't worry," Jason said. "We'll take the Gator. I

also have some aerial shots you can take back to the office."

As Jason and the Realtor left the room, Juliana went back to the work at hand. The men had no more than stepped out the back door when her cell phone rang. It was her mother.

"Hi, honey. A Mr. Alex Montgomery from La Galleria called looking for you."

Juliana had expected Loren, her boss, to call about Jason's purchase, but not Alex. "What did he have to say?"

"Your paintings sold. He wanted to know where to mail your commission check."

"On my last day at work, I left your address and phone number. I instructed my boss to mail my checks to you. So there was no reason for Alex to call and ask." In fact, she'd gone so far as to change her cell number so he couldn't contact her directly. In spite of what she'd told him, he'd had some crazy idea that she might want to see him again anyway—on the sly, of course. And to protect her reputation. As if she'd consider such a thing.

"I'm sorry," her mom said. "You told me that you left on good terms, so I couldn't understand why you wouldn't want to take his call."

A wave of nausea rolled through Juliana's tummy, threatening to send her rushing to the bathroom. But she swallowed it down and cleared her throat. "You didn't tell Alex where he could find me, did you?"

"No, but he seemed so kind and pleasant on the phone. I thought you'd be eager to talk to him yourself, especially since he has a buyer interested in purchasing more of your paintings."

Alex was a charmer, all right. And he'd just sweet-talked her mother into doing exactly what Juliana had asked her not to do. If she'd had a heart-to-heart with her mom when she'd first returned home, her mother would have understood and given him heck—in a pious way, of course. But Juliana hadn't leveled with her yet.

It wasn't like she planned to keep the baby a secret forever. She'd tell her mom the truth—every bit of it. She just wanted to wait until she was settled in Houston and could prove that she'd be all right, that she wouldn't need a husband or a father for her baby.

"I didn't want Alex to contact me here at the Rayburn ranch," Juliana said. "I'd prefer not to talk about my future work while I'm committed to another project."

Okay, so that was only partially true.

"But honey, isn't it great? One man took all three of your paintings, and Mr. Montgomery thinks he can sell him more."

What neither Alex nor her mother knew was that she could sell that same buyer paintings directly—and without a commission—if he actually had reason to stage another ranch house for potential buyers. But Jason Rayburn wasn't interested in her style of art. Not for himself, anyway.

"I hope you're not upset with me," her mother added.

How could Juliana ever be mad at her mom? The woman was practically a saint and had a heart of gold. "No, it's okay."

"So how is the job on the ranch going?"

"It's coming along fine. I should be done soon, then I'll search for work in the city."

"I wish you'd reconsider and look for a job around Brighton Valley. I'm sure you can find something here. I can post an ad in the church bulletin to see if anyone in the congregation is aware of an opening."

Just what the church secretary needed her daughter to do—parade herself around town, unwed, barefoot and pregnant. Sure, times had changed. Not everyone would point their fingers at her. But her mom didn't need to be embarrassed about Juliana's short sight when it came to choosing a mate worthy of a lifetime commitment.

"I actually have a few potential job opportunities already," Juliana said. "And they're all in the city. But I'll let you know if I need your help."

A double click sounded, letting her know another call was coming through. She took a peek at the display. Sure enough, it was Alex's cell number. She'd love to let it go to voice mail, but he'd just keep trying until she answered.

"Listen, Mom, that's Alex now."

"I'm sorry for letting him know how to contact you."

"That's okay. I love you. Talk to you soon." Then she switched over to the incoming call.

"Hey," he said when she answered. "Why did you change your number? You weren't avoiding me, were you, baby?"

"Just looking for a brand-new start. That's all."

"No need to do that. Listen, I'm not sure if your

mother told you or not, but I sold all three of those paintings. The buyer loves your work. How soon can you bring me something else?"

"I'm not interested in working with La Galleria."

"But I have a buyer on the hook. You're losing money by dragging your feet and being stubborn."

"So be it."

He paused a moment, as if plotting his next move. "Did you take care of…the little problem?"

The jerk. "I took care of it." But not the way he'd expected her to. She'd gone to see a doctor and was due to have a baby girl in late December. And she would continue to take care of *her* daughter for as long as she needed her. "Not to worry, Alex. All is well."

"Good. I'll be happy to reimburse you. Let me know how much you need."

"I don't need anything from you. *Ever.* Not a dime, not a phone call, not anything."

"But what about the buyer? I have his name, remember?"

"And I'm not interested. *Remember?*"

Then she did what she should have done the moment she'd heard his voice the very first time he'd asked for a date and suggested they keep it their "special little secret."

She hung up the phone and disconnected the line.

On Monday afternoon, Jason left Ian and the boys painting the barn and drove into town to pick up a few supplies at the hardware store. He'd noticed the engine knocking a couple of times on the way in and thought he ought to stop by Harv's Auto Repair and have him take a look at it.

If he were going to keep the ranch, he'd actually consider buying a new truck since this one was nearly twenty years old and had more than its share of wear and tear. The odometer showed fourteen thousand miles, but it had clearly made at least one lap around—maybe two.

After picking up the items on his list, he returned to the truck. But when he turned the key in the ignition, the damn thing wouldn't start. The lights worked, so he knew it wasn't the battery. He sat behind the wheel for a moment, then blew out a sigh.

Moments later, he'd dialed 4-1-1 and had Harvey Dennison on the line. "This is Jason Rayburn from the Leaning R. I'm parked on Main Street in the old Dodge pickup, but I can't get it to even turn over. Can you come out and have a look at it? I think it might be the starter."

"Nope. That's not it. We replaced that a couple of weeks ago. It's also got a new battery and an alternator. I'll come and bring the tow truck."

"So you're familiar with the engine?"

"Yep. Told your great-grandma it was time to buy a new one, but she passed on before she could do that." The mechanic blew out a sigh. "By the way, son, I'm sorry for your loss. Rosabelle Rayburn was a fine woman."

"Thank you." Not many days went by that he didn't hear someone in town tell him how much they thought of Granny. "Do you have any idea what's wrong with the truck?"

"I worked on it a couple of times for Ian. Told him what I told Mrs. Rayburn. But he said your daddy wasn't going to put any more money into the ranch. I'll do my best to fix it one more time, but it's going to need a new engine. That's for sure."

"Well, do what you need to do. I'm parked about two doors down from the hardware store. Since no one's going to steal it, I'll leave the keys on the floorboard."

"All righty, son. I'll be there in about an hour."

At least Jason wouldn't have to worry about getting a parking ticket, but he was stuck in town until he found a ride home.

He hated to bother Ian, who was knee-deep in the corral repair and overseeing the boys' painting. So he dialed the house.

Juliana answered on the third ring.

"Hey, it's me," he said. "The truck broke down while I was in town. Can you come and get me?"

"Sure. Where are you?"

"On Main Street, by the hardware store. But if you haven't had lunch yet, you can meet me at Caroline's. I'll wait to order until you get there."

Silence stretched across the line.

"What's the matter?" he asked. "Did you already eat?"

"No. It's just that I...well, I was trying to stay out of the public eye since I've started to show."

And Caroline's was a gathering place for the locals.

"If you feel better about it, I can order take-out and

meet you at the car when you arrive. But why don't you come on in? You aren't showing all that much yet. Besides, I doubt anyone will notice anything except how pretty you are."

He hoped she didn't think he was feeding her a line—or trying to sweet-talk her into doing him this favor. Every time he looked at her, he forgot she was pregnant. And when he remembered, he actually found it amazing to imagine a little one growing there.

"All right," she said. "But I can't get there for at least a half hour. Maybe a bit more."

"No problem. I'll wait for you at Caroline's."

After disconnecting the line, he crossed the street and entered the local diner. The lunch crowd was long gone, which ought to make Juliana happy. Her pregnancy was apparent to him now that he knew, but he couldn't imagine that anyone else would spot it so easily, especially since she wore loose clothing.

He suspected she'd be a loving mother. And while her child wouldn't have a father, Juliana would more than make up for that loss.

"I'll be right with you," Margie called from the kitchen. "But feel free to take a seat anywhere you want."

He had his choice of chairs at the counter or any of the tables, but before he could take a step toward a corner booth, Shannon Miller entered the diner.

Braden's mother seemed surprised to see him, although she had to know he was in town. She'd always been an attractive woman, a shapely brunette with green eyes and a sprinkle of freckles across her nose.

From what Jason had heard, she'd been a real knockout as a teenager, but she'd downplayed her beauty after she'd had Braden.

She'd only been eighteen at the time, which made her about forty-five now. Her hair didn't have any gray, although he wasn't sure if that was because of her age, her genes or her hairdresser.

"Hello, Jason." She offered him a smile. "I heard you were back in Brighton Valley."

"Good to see you, Shannon." He'd like to talk to her, to ask some of the questions he had for Braden. Maybe he should he invite her to join him. "Are you meeting someone?"

"No, I only stopped by to pick up some of Megan's muffins. I'm hosting my book club tomorrow morning and don't have time to bake anything myself."

"They must taste good if you drove all the way into town to buy them."

"They are. But this wasn't my only stop. I had to meet with the family attorney and make sure everything is in order. My dad has been pretty sick, but I didn't know how serious it was until now. He's been keeping it to himself."

Her smile faded, leaving her looking worn, troubled. After Jason had talked to Ralph Nettles earlier and learned about the conversation the men had had at the oncologist, Jason had connected the dots and assumed the worst.

Did Braden know? Maybe not, because if he did, he'd probably come home and leave the Camilla Cruz mystery alone, at least for the time being. He'd always been close to his mom and his granddad.

Jason had never really talked at length to Braden's mother. He'd told himself that he'd never had a reason to. He supposed that's because he felt as if he'd be disloyal if he did. But he wasn't sure to whom. His mom, maybe? His dad? Himself?

But Shannon Miller seemed like a nice woman who'd been through a lot — thanks to his father. And now she was facing more trouble. Besides, she might have some answers for those questions he hadn't been able to ask Braden.

"Can I buy you a cup of coffee?" he asked.

She paused for a moment, then said, "Yes, I'd like that. Thanks."

He led her to the corner booth he'd been eyeing before. They'd no more than taken a seat when Margie arrived with a carafe of coffee and filled both mugs that had been waiting on the table for the next diners.

"With your father sick and Braden gone, you must be pretty stretched," Jason said.

She sighed and tucked a loose strand of hair behind her ear. "It's been tough. I've been tempted to call Braden and let him know about my dad, but I haven't done it yet."

Good luck trying to get through to him, Jason thought. "Did he tell you why he went to Mexico?"

"He wanted to find out what Charles…or rather, your dad, had been doing there."

Jason knew that much. "Do you know anything about a woman named Camilla Cruz?"

"Just that she was Reuben Montoya's daughter."

Granny's previous foreman? The news took a moment to register. Jason knew Reuben well, but he'd never met Camilla. Or, if he had, he didn't remember her.

"Why do you want to know about Camilla?" Shannon asked.

"Because that's who Braden was looking for in Mexico. At least, he was following Dad's trail, and that's who Dad was looking for."

Her brow furrowed, but she didn't speak. Instead, she lifted her mug and took a sip of coffee.

"Do you have any idea why Dad would have been looking for Camilla?" Jason asked, prodding.

"No, other than the fact that she was young and beautiful."

Jason knew what Shannon was implying. Charles Rayburn liked pretty women. But something told Jason the mystery wasn't that simple. His father had never had to chase after a woman before or hire a PI to find her. Jason would be more inclined to think the woman had stolen something from him and he'd wanted it back.

"Did Braden mention anything to you about Dad hiring a private investigator?"

Shannon took another sip of coffee. "Braden's pretty tight-lipped."

"Even with you?"

She smiled. "Your brother is a man of few words, but when he speaks, it's from the heart. Genetically speaking, he received the finest qualities of both sides of the family."

Jason had to chew on that for a minute. Was that a loving mother defending her son? Or was it the truth?

Sadly, he didn't know Braden well enough to determine the answer for himself.

Shannon reached out and placed her hand over the top of his. "I'll bet you received the best qualities of both your parents, too, Jason."

Their gazes met, and he saw something warm and tender in hers. Something kind and almost…loving? Not that he wasn't happy to hear her say it—or that he didn't want to believe her. But at the same time, the unexpected words and maternal touch unbalanced him.

"I didn't know your mother very well," Shannon added, "but I was sorry to hear of her death. I felt somewhat responsible, although I think we were both victims in a sense."

"I felt responsible, too," Jason admitted, "even though I was only ten. Dad had me in therapy for a while, and I came to realize she made her own choices. She could have taken her medication and seen her psychiatrist regularly. She'd had issues long before Dad and you…" He paused, not wanting to point fingers at her or anyone. There wasn't anything anyone could do to fix things now. It was all in the past.

"I was young and rebellious back then. And I made a mistake. But fortunately, I didn't compound it by marrying Charles."

"He asked you?"

"Yes, after your parents' divorce. But I realized he didn't really love me. I'm not sure he was able to fully love anyone. But while I'm sorry about the scandal and the embarrassment it caused my parents and Granny, I'm not sorry about the pregnancy. Braden turned out to be a real blessing in my life, and I have no idea what I'd do without him."

When she withdrew her hand, a sense of loss threatened to leave Jason more unbalanced than ever.

A couple of times, when he'd been at Granny's for Christmas, Braden's mom had sent gifts to him and Carly. His sister had always accepted hers happily. But Jason hadn't known what to do with his, especially since Shannon often gave him things like board games that were meant to be played by two or more.

Had she been trying to encourage the two brothers to play together, to become friends? Looking back, as an adult, it seemed that way.

He wondered why she'd never married. He could see why she wouldn't accept his father's proposal. But had there ever been another special man in her life? He wouldn't ask, of course, but he was curious.

Granny had said that Shannon had devoted her life to Braden and then, after her mama had died, to her daddy. And if Granny had been embarrassed or upset by the scandal, she hadn't held it against either Braden or his mom. She'd always had a loving heart—and a forgiving nature.

"I'm sorry that my father wasn't the man he should have been," Jason said.

"It's not your fault. You can't make up for his short-comings."

Like making a lifetime commitment to a marriage, he supposed. Or to a woman in general.

"Your father saw his value in his success," she added. "But there's more to life than money, stock holdings and property. There's love and family."

"That's true, but you can't live on love alone. You do have to be able to pay the mortgage."

"I agree," she said. "And while your father had his faults, he had good qualities, too. He had a love for children, even if he didn't spend any time with his own. He financially supported many organizations that benefited underprivileged kids."

Jason agreed. "It would have been nice to have had more of his time, but you're right. He always did have a soft spot for kids. And he put his money where his mouth was."

"He also sent his child support checks regularly. Some men aren't that generous or supportive. Braden could have had it much worse."

It sounded as if Braden might have had it much better than Jason had. He'd had less of Charles, more of Granny—and a mother who'd loved him. Shannon had also lived long enough to be there for him. And unlike Carly's mom, Shannon hadn't put her dream of being on the stage ahead of her child.

Braden was lucky to have her.

Something told Jason that Juliana's baby would be just as fortunate. All she'd be missing was the financial support.

But maybe it was best if they steered clear of the touchy subjects, like Charles Rayburn. So Jason let the conversation drift naturally to a reminiscence of Braden as a child and Granny, who'd been as loving and maternal as Shannon.

Still, he continued to glance at the door, waiting for Juliana, who took much longer to arrive than the estimated thirty minutes. But Jason didn't mind. Not when he finally saw her walk in.

She'd taken time to style her hair, although the curls still fell long and loose along her shoulders. She'd also put on makeup. Apparently, his comment about looking pretty had caused her to take some extra time with her appearance. Not that she didn't set his heart racing in faded jeans and bare feet.

As she swept into the small-town eatery in her yellow sundress and a pair of sandals, he had an almost overwhelming urge to take her in his arms and welcome her with a hug and a kiss.

And while he managed to tamp down the sudden impulse to embrace her, he couldn't seem to wipe the silly smile from his face as he stood and made room for her to join him and Shannon at the booth.

Juliana had expected to find Jason seated at a table waiting for her, but she hadn't expected to see him having coffee with Braden's mother.

Apparently, by the look on her face, Shannon Miller was taken by surprise, too.

"I'm sorry I'm late," Juliana said as she slid into the corner booth.

"No problem." Jason returned to his seat.

Shannon didn't say a word, but she lifted a brow.

"I've been working for Mr. Rayburn," Juliana told her.

"And doing a great job," Jason added. "I don't know what I'd do without her."

"Your mother told me that you'd been laid off at the art gallery in Wexler," Shannon said. "I was sorry to hear that. I know how much you liked your job."

Not as much as she'd wanted to continue her education, but that would have to wait until the baby was older. "I'll be moving to Houston soon and will find something similar to do there."

"You don't have anything lined up yet?" Shannon clasped both hands around her mug. "Shouldn't you wait until you have a job before you leave your friends and family behind?"

"I have something in the works," Juliana said, although that wasn't quite true. She hoped Jason would put in a good word for her at Rayburn Energy. But if not, she'd find something else. How hard could it be?

But just in case, she probably should start an online job search when she got back to the ranch.

"Thanks for the coffee," Shannon said as she slid out from the booth. "I really enjoyed our chat, Jason. I hope you'll stop by the ranch while you're in town. You're always welcome."

"I'll do that."

She went to the cash register, where Margie rang up an order she'd boxed for her.

"I meant what I told Shannon," Jason said. "You've

been a huge help to me, Juliana. I know you said you think it's best if you moved on, but I'm going to tempt you to stay."

The *temptation* was what made her want to leave. As their gazes met and locked, there was no reason to explain because whatever buzzed between them kicked up again, making conversation unnecessary.

A grin tugged at one side of his lips. "I guess that wasn't the right word. What I meant to say is that I'd like to make you an offer you can't refuse."

She couldn't help but smile. "I'm almost afraid to ask what it is."

"The way I see it, we only have another week or two of packing left. I'd like to offer you a bonus if you'll stick it out and finish."

"You're paying me enough as it is, so you don't need to do that."

"I know. But I want to."

She'd prefer a position at one of his businesses in Houston. Would she be out of line if she asked?

"I'm going to provide a nursery for you," he said.

She glanced to her right and left, hoping no one in the diner had heard him. Had he forgotten that she hadn't wanted word of her pregnancy to get out?

"What's the matter?" he asked.

The diner was empty, which he apparently knew. And Margie was nowhere in sight. But still, her secret was too precious to risk.

She leaned forward, narrowed her eyes and whispered, "Would you please lower your voice?"

"No one heard me. And that's all I plan to say."

"*I* heard you."

"I've been watching the door and can assure you no one is within twenty feet of us."

She blew out a sigh, not appeased. "To answer your question, I'll consider staying. But the bonus you offered is out of the question."

"Why not? The stuff you're going to need will be expensive, and—"

"That's *enough*! We'll talk about that later."

Now it was his turn to look around the diner and check for eavesdropping waitresses or townspeople, although the place was still empty and Margie had yet to return from the kitchen.

He didn't say anything more, and she was finally able to mull around his offer. His generosity was touching—and unexpected. Yet she couldn't help but be offended by it, too. It felt as if he was trying to buy her.

But the move was going to be costly. And so was preparing for a baby. Why couldn't she just accept it as a bonus and go on?

"Do you want to eat?" he asked.

"Not unless we can change the subject."

"Deal."

Good. A temporary reprieve from the problem at hand. She could think about the dilemma as well as both temptations—the man and his over-the-top financial offer—later.

With the issue temporarily tabled, another cropped up when Margie approached with two menus.

"Well, what a nice surprise," the waitress said.

"Looks like that new job turned into an unexpected... *friendship*."

Her wink suggested that the town rumor mill was already cranked up and ready for action.

Chapter Eight

They'd no more than started back to the ranch in Juliana's white Honda Civic when Jason addressed the elephant in the room—or rather, seated on the console between them. "I wouldn't have mentioned the word *nursery* if I hadn't been absolutely sure there was no one around who could hear me."

"I realize that now," Juliana said as she drove down the tree-shaded main drag of town. "And I'm sorry for freaking out, but it threw me into panic mode. I wasn't sure why you brought it up in the diner—or how much more you were going to say."

"That's all I was going to bring up. And I realize you want to tell your mother and grandmother first. But the baby isn't going to get any smaller. How long are you going to keep this a secret?"

"Until I'm settled in Houston and can assure them that I'm doing well."

Jason studied her stiff form as she gripped the wheel and stared straight ahead. It really wasn't any of his business when she told people, but it seemed to him that she was *afraid* to tell.

"Will they be angry with you?" he asked.

"They'll be...disappointed."

"Because you're not married?" In this day and age, he'd think that people would be more accepting of that sort of thing.

"Yes, but the details behind it are so...embarrassing. I *never* would have gotten involved with a married man. Or a liar, for that matter. But Alex led me to believe... Well, I could blame him for being a jerk, but I fell for it. I should have been more skeptical."

"I'd think that most people assume they can trust their partner. And that may not always be the case."

He wondered whom she was really trying to protect—her mother? Or herself? But he didn't think it was up to him to assume the role of her shrink.

"Maybe someday I'll find a man I can trust."

"I'm sure you will." At least, he hoped she would. She deserved the white-picket-fence dream and everything that came with it. "And that brings me back to my offer. Buying a crib and setting up a nursery will be expensive. And I can afford to help."

"I have a little money put away, so it won't break me. Besides, I plan to go to a thrift shop and pick up a secondhand crib."

He reached across the seat and trailed his fingers

along her arm, felt her tremble at the touch. Yet she didn't pull away.

Did she realize he'd come to care about her, to want the very best for her and her baby? That he'd…be the friend she needed in her corner?

Right. Because friendship makes your blood heat every damn time she walks into a room.

Shrugging off the unbidden thought, he insisted, "I have faith in you. I know you can handle anything life throws your way. But you'll have to do it on your own, and it'll be a struggle—no matter how capable you are. So why *not* accept help when you can?"

She merely stared at the road ahead. After a couple of beats, she glanced across the seat. When their eyes met, tears had gathered in hers, making them glossy.

"Did Braden's mom have anything to do with you making that offer?" she asked.

The question caught him by surprise. "Does Shannon know you're pregnant?"

Juliana, who'd turned back to watch the road, shot another glance his way, her eyes wide, all signs of tears gone. "No! You're the only one who knows about that. And now I wish I hadn't said anything at all."

"I'm sorry you feel that way."

She veered slightly to the right to correct their course, then shook her head. "You still didn't answer my question about Braden's mom."

"Why would she have anything to do with my offer?" He paused, realizing what Juliana might be implying.

Both women had gotten pregnant by married men.

And while Shannon had gone through her childbirth and motherhood with the support of her parents and was able to live out on the ranch, away from town, Juliana was heading to the city—on her own.

Of course, Juliana had a widowed mother and grandmother in her corner, if she ever told them she was expecting, but he doubted either of them had the financial resources to allow her to stay at home and take care of her baby. She'd have to get a job and find reliable day care.

"I'm sorry," she said, "it's just that I'm having a difficult time sorting through the motive of such an overwhelmingly generous offer. Do you really want me as an employee that badly?"

"Yes, I do. But it's more than that."

"What is it, then? Are you a white knight determined to help unwed, pregnant damsels in distress?"

As the accusation tore into his conscience, he turned in his seat and faced her profile. So he'd been right. *That's* what she'd meant about Braden's mother having something to do with his offer.

Shannon had told him he couldn't make up for his father's shortcomings, something he already knew. Now Juliana seemed to be suggesting the same thing. "Can't I just be a nice guy?" he asked.

"Yes, and I'm sorry for sounding so skeptical. I'm afraid my experience with Alex has left me with a bit of scar tissue. Besides, I'm vulnerable right now, and it would be easy to mislabel any feelings I might have."

"I can understand that." He supposed, in some ways, they were both damaged goods. But this was one subject he'd rather let drop, at least if it was going to poke at any excess baggage he might have.

"By the way," he said, "Shannon's father isn't doing well. Apparently, it's serious enough that she's thinking about asking Braden to come home from Mexico."

"Hopefully she can get a hold of him if she needs him."

Jason thought on that for a moment. "I'd like to do something for her, although I'm not sure what. Do you think they need money?"

"Probably, but Braden has access to his trust fund, doesn't he? So they should be okay financially. Besides, just telling Braden that you're sorry and letting him know that he can call on you if he needs anything would go a long way."

She had a point. Their father had set up separate trust funds for each of his children years ago, money they could use to attend college, purchase a house or spend as they saw fit. And as trustee to the family trust, Jason had added more to those trusts according to the instructions in the document.

But Jason felt compelled to offer to help anyway. And while throwing cash at the first sign of a problem was the kind of thing their father might do, it really didn't sit right with him. Some people needed a pat on the back, a hug or a heartfelt word.

Jason had been one of them, especially when he was a kid.

So why did it seem easier to offer money than a kind word? Had he been too emotionally damaged to see the forest for the trees? As much as he liked to think he'd grown up to be different from his father, it certainly seemed that way.

Rather than stir up any more deep-rooted memories, he kept quiet for the rest of the ride back to the ranch.

After Juliana parked near the barn, they climbed from the Honda. Instead of heading to the house with her, he turned toward the barn. "Thanks for the ride home. I need to talk to Ian and check on the boys."

"I'll be working in the guest room where your father stayed. That's what I was doing when you called. There wasn't much to inventory or pack, so I expect to be finished soon. It's nice to move on to a new room. It makes me feel as though I'm making progress."

Did that mean she planned to stick around until the job was done? He hoped so.

The truth was, he could find a qualified replacement fairly soon, especially if he called the home office and asked Doug to send someone out from Houston.

But when all was said and done, he didn't want to work with anyone else. He and Juliana had become a team. And he liked having her around—more than he cared to admit.

Juliana's talk with Jason left her just as unsettled as ever about staying on the ranch and completing her job assignment. Not only was her cowboy boss gorgeous, she could imagine him in a business suit heading an executive board meeting with grace and style. And his generosity was making it impossible to think of him as the type of man she needed to avoid.

Still, as she proceeded to the guest room to finish

the packing she'd started earlier today, she couldn't make sense of it. He was already paying her far more than that type of temporary position called for. Why?

Was it because he felt sorry for his sister's down-and-out friend and this was a way of doling out charity and having her think she had somehow earned it?

Or was there a trust factor involved? She was handling the family heirlooms and personal possessions, which held sentimental value, which could make the job worth more to him than an hourly wage.

Of course, there was another possibility, something she hadn't considered. He'd said he was too busy to do the inventory himself. And that certainly appeared to be true. But what if it was more than that? What if the task was too difficult, emotionally speaking, for him to tackle on his own?

No, that couldn't be it. Unlike Braden and Carly, selling the ranch didn't seem to bother Jason at all. So maybe he didn't have a sensitive streak.

Then again, he wanted to do something for Braden's mother, which was sweet. Maybe, like he'd said, he was just a nice guy and wanted to do something kind for her and the baby.

That being the case, it had been rude of her to turn him down—at least, after she'd implied that he had ulterior motives for making such a generous offer.

She blew out a sigh. But hadn't she thought the best of Alex? Hadn't she believed his lies and reasons for keeping their relationship a secret?

We don't want anyone thinking that I'm using you to cinch the deal to purchase half the gallery. And once

I'm a co-owner, we don't want anyone to think you're vying for extra perks. Let's keep things special and private—just between the two of us.

Yeah, right. He hadn't wanted his wife to get wind of his shenanigans. And he hadn't wanted anyone to tell Juliana about his marital status. She should have seen a red flag then, but she hadn't.

She snatched the packing tape from the top of the bed, then sealed the cardboard box she'd filled right before Jason had called asking for a ride home from town.

With the closet and dresser drawers empty, she moved on to the nightstands. There wasn't much to enter on her spreadsheet—a book by James Patterson, two business magazines, a travel guide of Mexico... Now, that was interesting, especially since this was the room Charles had stayed in last.

She set the reading material aside and reached for a red flashlight, which was missing a piece in back. As she pulled it from the drawer, one of the batteries fell out on the floor and rolled under the bed. She laid the other parts on top of the comforter, then dropped to her knees and peered under the ruffled bed skirt to retrieve the runaway battery.

Instead, she spotted a blue plastic container the size of a shoebox. She slid it out and studied it, wondering what it was doing there.

Since her job was to go through every nook and cranny in the house to determine which items should be kept and which should be thrown out, she popped open the lid. Inside she found several invoices, a letter and copies of an agreement for the lease of a storage unit in San Antonio, as well as the key.

It didn't take long to realize she'd uncovered a clue to the mystery Jason and Braden were trying to solve.

The invoices were in both Spanish and English. It appeared that they were from a Mexican art dealer to Charles Rayburn for the delivery of several paintings and statues.

The storage locker in San Antonio belonged to Charles, too, and he'd paid for it a year in advance.

At the sound of the front door opening and closing, Juliana called out, "Jason? Can you please come here? I found something you need to see."

Moments later, he entered the guest room, tall and lean—a Texas cowboy on the outside, but a wealthy businessman to the bone. "What's up?"

"Look what someone stashed under the bed." She got to her feet and handed him the box.

"What's this?"

"Your father was involved with an art dealer in Mexico and apparently took possession of some paintings and statues. He also seems to have a storage unit in San Antonio. From the size of it, he must have planned to buy and sell those pieces in the States."

"I don't understand. He never said a word about it to me. And we usually met for lunch on Wednesdays." As Jason riffled through the box, his brow furrowed, Juliana inhaled his woodsy scent. She watched his expression morph from confusion to disbelief to...disappointment?

"Do you think Braden knows about this?" he asked.

"I have no idea, but he must have stumbled onto something. I wonder if Camilla Cruz has anything to do with it."

"She must—if my dad was looking for her." Jason set the box on the bed, then crossed his arms and gazed at Juliana. "Do you think they could have been involved in anything illegal?"

"Anything is possible, but those invoices appear legitimate to me. They talk about art sales and shipments, so I think it's on the up-and-up."

"Braden has to know something. Could he and my dad have been involved in an import business? It doesn't seem likely, but he knew Reuben, Camilla's father. So he must know her, too. And if he has a stake in it, he might be down there trying to tie up loose ends."

An expression crossed his face, like a boy who'd found out all his friends had been invited to a campout and he'd been excluded.

She placed her hand on his back, felt the heat of his body, the bulk of his muscle as it quickened and tightened with her touch. "There's only one way to find out. You'll have to ask Braden when he gets home."

"There's a faster way than that." He tossed her an impish grin. "We can drive to EZ Storage in San Antonio, find unit number four-twenty-two, use this key and have a look ourselves."

We? He was including her in the Rayburn family mystery? "You want me to go with you?"

"You're the art expert, aren't you?"

Her hand trailed down his back, lingering a

moment before she removed it completely. "I wouldn't say that, exactly."

"You know a lot more about the subject than I do."

That might be true. "But what if it turns out to be a wild goose chase?"

"Then we end up having a nice dinner and a stroll along the Riverwalk. We might even get a chance to see Carly's show—if she's working. Besides, as long as I'm stewing about this thing, I'm not going to be able to focus on anything else. So pack your bags. We'll leave first thing in the morning."

She probably ought to be a little uneasy about taking such a long drive with him—and spending the night. But she couldn't help the zing of excitement that rose up inside her. And it wasn't entirely due to uncovering a mystery that now included art dealers and paintings. And while she knew better than to let her thoughts wander in too far of a romantic direction, she wasn't sure what he had in mind.

"Are you springing for two rooms?" she asked.

"Sure."

Then he winked, sending that little zing soaring.

Nice guy? Or handsome CEO with an ulterior motive?

"Can you be ready to leave by eight?" he asked.

When he smiled, in spite of any apprehension her brain tossed out in warning, her heart did a swan dive in her chest.

And she found herself nodding—and planning what to take on an overnight trip.

* * *

The next morning, Jason showered and packed. After brewing a pot of coffee, he poured himself a cup, then took it into the den while he emailed the home office. He had to tell his staff that he'd be traveling for the next thirty-six hours or so and that he'd have limited availability if they needed him. Doug, his right-hand man, could handle things in his absence.

Since he had an address for EZ Storage but no idea where to find it, he also wanted to check Mapquest to determine the best exit he should take off the interstate.

When the house phone rang, he reached for the receiver, although he was more focused on the computer screen than the person who was calling. So he answered with a rather ambivalent "Hello."

At the sound of his sister's voice, he released the mouse, sat back in his chair and perked up. "Hey, Carly. How's the singing gig?"

"So far, so good. But how are things at the ranch? Did you ever get a chance to talk to Juliana?"

"Yes, and I hired her. You were right. She's doing a great job."

"I'm glad to hear it. That makes me feel better about leaving you in a lurch."

At least Carly seemed somewhat sympathetic to his plight. "Do you feel any better about me listing the ranch?"

"I still hate the idea of letting it go, but the truth is, I can't be there all the time."

"And neither can I—or Braden."

"Speaking of Braden, he called me early this morning. His grandpa was hospitalized yesterday afternoon. It's pretty serious, so Braden is coming home sooner than he planned. He asked if I'd set up a family meeting this weekend or soon afterward."

Damn—it seemed as though Braden was in for a real shock when he arrived. A pang of sympathy for his brother struck hard. "I'm sorry to hear about his grandfather. I'll check in on his mom and see if she needs anything."

"Gosh, Jason. That'd be really sweet. I'm sure she'd appreciate it, especially if Braden can't get back right away."

"What would stop him?"

"I'm not sure, but he's in some small village and has to catch a ride to a bus stop. Then it's nine hours to the nearest airport."

"Where's his truck?"

"When I asked, he told me it was a long story."

Well, that was one Jason would definitely like to hear, along with a few others. "So when are you available for that meeting?"

"I'm off on Mondays. I'll see what I can work out. I assume we'll meet at the Leaning R."

"That's probably best. And just so you know, I'll clear my calendar on any day you two can swing that meeting."

"I'll ask Braden how next Monday will work for him and let you know."

Silence filled the line, then Carly asked, "Is Ian still working for you?"

"Yes, why?"

"I don't know. I thought he might have gotten tired of holding things together on the ranch without any family support."

The same thing had crossed Jason's mind, but the guy didn't seem to be one to give up easily. "Well, for what it's worth, he has my support now."

Again, she paused. "I'm not sure if he told you, but he'd be willing to supervise the Leaning R if we wanted to keep things going. At least, that's what he told me a while back."

Jason didn't respond. He knew how Carly felt about selling the ranch to strangers, but that didn't solve the problem of having a family member live on the property—or having to spend the better part of his or her life there.

"You can ask around," she added, "but from what I gathered, Ian knows cattle. And Granny thought the world of him."

Jason had asked around. The vet and a few neighboring ranchers spoke highly of the man. And even if the three siblings decided they could trust Ian to run things for them, holding on to the Leaning R meant meeting regularly with Braden and Carly. And before Jason could even comprehend something like that, he'd have to see how things played out on Monday.

After telling Carly goodbye, he returned his focus to the screen, made a mental note of the exit he'd have to take, then shut down the laptop. He'd no more than risen from his seat when Juliana walked in.

"Who was on the phone?" she asked.

"Carly. She said Mr. Miller is in the hospital and

Braden is coming home early. We've tentatively set up a family meeting next Monday."

"Does that mean we're not going to San Antonio?"

"On the contrary. I'm just as eager to see what's in that storage unit. The more information I have about my dad's trip to Mexico and his search for Camilla, the better prepared I'll be for that meeting."

She nodded, then leaned against the doorjamb.

Damn, she was beautiful, with the mass of red curls tumbling along her shoulders and those golden-brown eyes. He scanned the length of her, the way she crossed her arms over the swell of her belly. He'd figured he might be turned off by her pregnancy, but instead, he found it appealing in an unexpected way.

"Do you know whether the baby is a boy or a girl?" he asked.

She blessed him with a bright-eyed smile, straightened and ran her hand over her womb. "It's a girl."

He returned her smile. "That's nice. I hope she has your hair."

"I hope so, too." Something about the way she smiled, the way her eyes sparkled, let him know she'd been imagining what the little girl would look like. And right this moment, he couldn't help getting caught up in that same wonder.

"Your hair is beautiful," he said. "I can see you two at the playground together—mother and daughter."

"You know, I really don't care what color her hair is. The reason I said that is because I'd like her to be all mine and not bear any resemblance to her father. But either way, I'm going to love her. In fact, I already do."

"She's going to be a lucky kid."

"Thanks. I'm also going to teach her to be honest and loving and kind. So even if she ends up looking like her dad, she won't be anything like him."

They stood like that for a moment, caught up in something tender and sweet—something he felt blessed to be a part of, although he wasn't quite sure what it was.

She gasped, then glanced down at her belly.

"What's the matter?" Jason moved toward her, afraid she'd suffered some kind of pain. Afraid something was wrong, that the little red-haired girl—or the blonde or brunette…did it even matter to him?—was in jeopardy.

Juliana looked up, her eyes wide, her lips parted. "She moved."

"The baby?" He eased closer yet.

"Yes, I'm sure that's what it was. The doctor said I might feel something soon—like the flutter of a butterfly's wing. And I just did."

His hand lifted. "Can I…?"

"Yes, of course. But I'm not sure if it's strong enough for you to feel anything yet."

He placed his hand on her tummy, felt the swell of her womb, the warmth of her body, the softness of her breath. And although he couldn't feel any movement whatsoever, he didn't draw away. He just stood there, caught up in her floral scent and in the intimacy of the moment.

And while he'd missed the miracle she'd just experienced, for some wild and crazy reason, he felt a part of it just the same.

Chapter Nine

Before leaving for San Antonio, Jason decided to stop by the Miller ranch.

He doubted Juliana would mind, but he ran the idea past her anyway.

"I'd feel bad if we left town without checking in on Shannon and her father first," Juliana said, "especially with Braden out of the country."

Ten minutes later, they drove into the Millers' yard just as Shannon was locking the front door, the strap of her black purse hanging over her shoulder.

"We didn't come to visit," Jason said as he and Juliana climbed from the car. "We just wanted to see how things were going."

Shannon stepped off the porch and met them in the yard. "The doctor admitted my dad to the hospital last night. He's in the ICU. I stayed there until just after dawn and came home to shower. You caught me as I was heading back."

"I'm sorry he isn't doing well," Juliana said. "Did Braden get home yet?"

"No, but he finally has better cell phone reception. The only problem is, his battery needs to be recharged, and he can't do that on a bus. But at least he'll be able to call again—eventually."

"How are you holding up?" Jason asked.

"I'm okay." Her red-rimmed eyes suggested otherwise.

Jason slipped his arm around Juliana. "Is there anything we can do to help?"

"That's nice of you to offer, but our foreman has things under control here. And Dad's doctor, Tom Hawthorne, is an old high school friend of mine. He's been very supportive, so we're in good hands."

Jason reached into his pocket and pulled out a business card. "Here's my contact information. Juliana and I will be out of town until tomorrow night, but if you need anything, let me know. I'll make sure it gets done."

"Thanks. I appreciate that." She tucked the card in her purse. "I'd better go. I'm hoping to talk to Tom when he makes his rounds this morning."

"Go ahead. We need to take off, too." Jason watched her head for her car, his arm still wrapped around Juliana. He wasn't sure why he continued to hold her close. It hadn't been a conscious move, although he supposed it was a sign of unity, of the team they'd become.

As Shannon slid behind the wheel of her silver Ford Taurus, Jason let his arm slide lower on Juliana's back until he slowly drew away.

"Come on," he said, "we'd better get on the road."

As they climbed into her car, neither of them said a word about him slipping his arm around her as if they were a couple. Just to make sure the subject didn't come up, he turned on the radio, and after a few miles, they fell into a casual conversation that lasted the rest of the six-hour drive.

When they arrived at EZ Storage in San Antonio, they had to ask for help in locating number 422. Come to find out it was a climate-controlled unit in a special building.

Using the key Juliana had found back at the ranch, they unlocked the door and gazed at the numerous paintings, ceramics and other Southwestern-style pieces of art that filled the unit.

"Wow," Jason said as he gazed at the stored items, each numbered and listed on invoices and checked off on a master list. He turned to Juliana, who seemed just as surprised as he was by the sight. "What do you think?"

"The paperwork seems to be in order, so it appears your father was involved in a legitimate import business—or at least he planned to be. Some of these things are high quality—and expensive. I'll use my connections to see if I can find out what he planned to do with them. If he was going to open up a shop or planned to sell them, I should be able to get more details for you."

"Are those connections at La Galleria?" Jason asked, hoping she wouldn't go through Alex.

"No. Fortunately, I've met a lot of people in the past two years who can help me."

He was glad to hear that. He'd rather hire an art expert or appraiser he didn't know than have Juliana cross paths with that jerk again.

As she continued to study the inventory, Jason walked through the storage unit, noting each of the paintings. Not all of them were signed by Camilla, but several were. One of hers sat away from the others. It was a portrait of two bright-eyed children—a boy and a girl about three years old—in front of a Christmas tree, loaded with presents. They were cute kids, and she'd captured something in their expressions—that same vivid, undefinable quality she'd captured in the portrait of Granny.

"Hey," Juliana said as she knelt beside a small box she'd found toward the rear of the storage unit. "Look at this."

He joined her and dropped to his knees beside her. "What'd you find?"

She lifted an envelope, showing him a letter she'd been reading. "It's from Camilla to your father."

"Were they involved in some kind of business venture?" he asked.

"Apparently, their relationship went much deeper than that." She handed him the note Camilla had written in a distinct, flowery script. "They were in love."

"That's hard to believe." He glanced at the letter,

then stared at the other envelopes inside the box. "My father never loved anyone but himself."

"I think these letters may prove otherwise."

He read the one she'd given him.

Dear Charles,

I'm sorry to leave in the middle of the night like this, but I had to go and didn't want to talk to you any more about my decision, especially in person.

It's not that I don't love you, because I do. But like I told you before, your history with women concerns me. I've been betrayed before, and I don't want to go through another heartbreaking divorce.

I so want to believe that what you say is true, that I'm different from the others, that you've never felt this way before, that you'll love me forever. You asked me to stay on the ranch and to give you time to prove it. I wish that I could, but I can't.

My sister is sick, and I have to go home. She has small children who need someone to look after them. Please understand. Perhaps at another time, I'll come back to Texas, and we can see if you feel the same way.

As for me? I love you and always will.

Camilla

"See what I mean?" Juliana asked. "He wanted to marry her, but she turned him down."

"I don't blame her. Look at his track record. I'd be

afraid, too, especially if I'd been betrayed and didn't want to go through a second divorce." Hell, as it was, Jason had been afraid to lower his guard and love the man, himself. And he was just his son.

Juliana leaned back, resting her bottom against her heels. "Well, either way, I find it sad and bittersweet."

"You mean because our internet search revealed that Camilla died two years ago?"

"That, too."

He studied her for a moment, the way she bit down on her bottom lip, the way she studied the other letters in the box. Then she turned to him, her pensive gaze filled with starry-eyed wonder. "Aren't you curious about whether they ever got back together? Whether he proved himself to her?"

Even after being betrayed and hurt by the man she once trusted with her heart, Juliana was still a hopeless romantic.

Jason cupped her cheek and smiled. "I can see why you would be, but he didn't marry her. So does that answer your question?"

"But he went looking for her in Mexico. And he was storing her paintings—and apparently buying them. I think there's a lot more to the story than meets the eye."

He brushed his thumb across her cheek, felt her silky-soft skin. She really did deserve to get married someday and to live happily ever after—if such a thing were even possible. But he wasn't sure if there was a man on earth who deserved her.

"I'm sure you're right," he said. "There's a lot we don't know." A lot they'd never know.

She placed her hand over his, holding their connection. "You're a good man, Jason Rayburn."

Was he? Deep inside, where he was reluctant to let even his own thoughts wander, he wanted to believe her, but he feared he was too much like his father—unable to love someone in the way they deserved to be loved.

Lord knew he tried his best to shake any similarities he might have to his father, any flaws in character he may have learned along the way, and he tried to do the right thing. So to have Juliana recognize his good qualities set off something warm and fluid in his soul.

Unable to help himself, he brushed a kiss across her lips—gentle at first, but the growing desire he felt whenever she was near took over, and he drew her close, running his hands up and down the slope of her back.

She pressed into him, and when her lips parted, his tongue swept inside her mouth. As the kiss intensified, passion threatened to explode right there in the rented storage shed.

Had he ever wanted another woman more?

When they came up for air, he continued to hold her close. His knees ached, yet he didn't want to let her go.

"What do you say we head to the hotel?" he whispered against her hair.

"We definitely need to get out of here." She drew back and got to her feet.

Her flushed cheeks suggested that she'd been just as aroused by the kiss as he was, but she cleared her throat and said, "That kiss may have given you the impression that I changed my mind about…things. But we do have two rooms, right?"

So much for her being as moved as he was.

"Yes," he said. "That was the deal."

He just hoped she didn't think he'd pulled a fast one when she found out that those two rooms were adjoining.

True to his word, Jason checked into two rooms at El Palacio, a five-star hotel with a view of the river.

While he was giving his credit card to the hotel clerk, Juliana wandered over to an impressive water fountain in the center of the lobby. It was an old-world style with a colorful tile mosaic undoubtedly made by artisan craftsmen.

Still, as she carried her overnight bag back to the registry desk, she marveled at the swanky lobby, the impressive decor and the courteous staff. Apparently, this was the way the rich and famous traveled. Not that she stayed in cheap accommodations, but El Palacio was in a class by itself.

When she approached Jason, he held the key cards in one hand and was returning his cell phone to his pocket with the other.

"I called Carly while you were checking out the fountain," he said. "I was hoping we could see her show, but she had to call in sick tonight. She has some kind of stomach bug, so she won't be performing."

"That's too bad. It would have been nice to see her on the stage. She has an awesome voice."

"I agree," he said. "So what do you want to do about dinner?"

"I'm pretty hungry, so anything sounds good."

"There's a steak house on the top floor with a view of the river. Why don't we try that?"

She'd brought the black dress he'd purchased for her. It actually fit, although it was formfitting in the waist, so her condition wouldn't be a secret. But who would know her six hours from Brighton Valley?

Thirty minutes later, she walked out of the bathroom, content with her appearance, just as a knock sounded on the adjoining door. When she opened it, Jason's eyes widened. He didn't speak right away, and she placed her hand on her tummy. "I'm sorry. Maybe I should wear the sundress."

"Please don't change. You look amazing."

"I know, but my pregnancy is so obvious. I feel a little—self-conscious."

"I understand why, since you haven't told your mother yet. But who's going to see you here? Besides, I think it's something to be proud of. You have that glow expectant mothers are supposed to have. I've never noticed it on other women, but you've definitely got it. Especially tonight."

Could she believe him? She certainly wanted to. And by the way his gaze caressed her, it was pretty hard not to.

She'd taken special care with her hair, pulling it up into a twist, which showed off the pearl earrings Grandpa had given her for her sixteenth birthday. She'd also put on some lipstick and mascara—nothing fancy.

When she'd looked in the bathroom mirror, she'd been pleased with her reflection—from the waist up, anyway.

To be honest, she was proud of the swell of her womb, the proof that her daughter was growing strong and healthy. But she'd been hiding it for so long…

Jason took her by the hand. "Come on. Let's go."

They left their rooms and took the elevator to the top floor, to Ernesto's, the steak house where Jason had made reservations for two.

The hostess, a tall brunette in her early forties, reached for two leather-bound menus and smiled. "Follow me, Mr. Rayburn." Then she led them to a linen-draped table with a view of the city lights and the river below.

Within minutes, a busboy had brought them water with lemon slices, as well as a variety of homemade breads and a small bowl of butter.

When the sommelier brought out the wine list, Juliana said, "I'll just have water. Thank you."

Jason chose a Napa Valley cabernet sauvignon and ordered it by the glass. When they were finally alone, he said, "Thanks for making the trip with me. It's not fun tackling family mysteries on your own."

She smiled. "A trip to a storage unit in San Antonio wasn't in my job description, but it did make for an exciting day."

"What did?" he asked. "Finding the love letters or the art?"

The kiss they shared had been pretty exciting, but she didn't dare mention that. Instead, she said, "I've always enjoyed a good romance novel, but it was fun to find those paintings, too."

"Then I'm glad working for me hasn't been entirely tedious."

"It hasn't. Even when I'm back at the ranch, I enjoy going through the family heirlooms and knickknacks. I almost feel as though I'm cheating someone out of the task."

"Not me. I have far too much to do. So you've taken a lot off my hands. And you've done an awesome job. I'm amazed at how organized you are."

And she was amazed at how generous he was. He'd given her a handsome salary—albeit for only three weeks' time. But he'd also offered to pay for her nursery, which was going above and beyond.

Was it a ploy? An attempt to manipulate her somehow?

Braden thought that Jason might be a charmer, like their father. But Jason didn't seem to emulate the man. Instead, he'd been skeptical of his dad's ability to truly love Camilla. And he didn't respect the man's womanizing.

No, the two men had to be different.

Besides, look how kind he'd been with Shannon. He'd wanted to check on her before leaving today. And he'd offered her his business card, saying he'd make sure she had anything she needed.

How sweet was that?

And while they'd been on the Miller ranch, talking to Shannon, Jason had slipped his arm around Juliana. Not only was that an affectionate gesture, it was also a move that let Shannon know that they were more than a boss and employee. It suggested they were also a couple.

When she'd told him she was pregnant, it hadn't seemed to faze him at all. In fact, he'd seemed to find the idea of her having a baby exciting. He'd gone so far as to touch her growing womb, hoping to feel a kick. He'd also mentioned her expectant glow tonight.

Did that mean he could actually grow to love her *and* her daughter?

Whoa. Juliana quickly took a sip of her icy water, cooling her heated blood and her racing fantasies. She was reading far more into this than was feasible. And she was setting herself up for a major heartbreak.

A waiter brought Jason's wine, interrupting her thoughts. Then the maître d' took their orders. Before long, their conversation resumed with safer topics and better things to think about.

"It's too bad we couldn't see Carly tonight," Juliana said. "She's always wanted to be on the stage, like her mother."

"I know. But I hope a singing career is her dream and not one her mother pushed her into."

It's funny that he'd say that when he'd followed in his father's footsteps. Maybe not in character, but in his career choice. Then again, someone had to take the helm of Rayburn Enterprises now that Charles was gone. And Jason was the one who'd been groomed for it.

After dinner, they ordered dessert—crème brûlée for her and chocolate lava cake for him.

Jason signed the bill and charged it to his room, then he stood and pulled out her chair.

"Thank you for dinner," she said. "It was wonderful."

"You're welcome. But it was the company and the ambience that made it special."

She thought so, too.

On the walk to the elevator she was tempted to slip her arm in his, but she refrained.

When the doors opened, they stepped inside and began the descent to the seventeenth floor. Jason's cologne, a woodsy scent laced with musk, taunted her, and she was again tempted to reach for him. But then what?

Would he expect more from her tonight?

As tempting as it might be to make love with him, she'd made up her mind that she wouldn't have sex again unless she was married. And that wasn't a conversation she was looking forward to having with him, especially since she was coming very close to falling in love with him and feared a discussion like that might scare him off.

And even if he didn't suggest sleeping together, she feared telling him how she felt about him. Her emotions were still too new to trust.

When the doors opened on the seventeenth floor, he took her hand and led her to her room.

"Do you have your key card?" he asked.

"Yes." She dug through her purse and pulled it out. "Right here."

When she let herself in, he followed her.

That didn't surprise her since they'd come out that

door, but things could get a little awkward now. Still, she'd find out just what he was expecting from her— and he'd learn what he could expect from her.

He took a seat on the edge of her bed. Okay, so he wasn't planning on making a mad dash to his room. Did he just expect to have an after-dinner chat?

She hoped so, because if he kissed her again, she just might weaken and forget her resolve about sex before marriage. And then where would she be?

"I've come to care for you," she admitted. "And we definitely have chemistry."

A crooked grin stretched across his face. "I care for you, too. And you're right about the chemistry."

Her heart began pounding in her chest like a runaway locomotive. He hadn't said a word to her about sex—and maybe didn't plan to. So why did she feel so compelled to make a speech?

She ran her hands along her hips, fidgeting just a moment, then pressed on. "Just so you know, I'm not going to make love with a man I'm not married to. I made that mistake once, but I'm not going to do it again."

His smile faded. "I can understand your concern, but I don't need a piece of paper to make a commitment to someone. If we make love, I'm not going to ditch you. I'll be a good lover, and I'll provide well for you."

If he thought that was going to appease her or make her feel better, he was wrong.

"I appreciate that, but it's not enough. I want more than a good lover and provider." She wanted a loving husband and father for her child, but Jason was a smart man. Surely he knew what she meant.

"I'm not the marrying kind," he said.

"Why do you say that?"

He paused for a beat. Was he wondering why he'd made the claim? Or did he want to choose the right words?

"I haven't seen any marriages that have had happy endings. And even if I had, I'm not sure that I have what it takes to make one work."

She appreciated his honesty and hoped that he wouldn't blame her for protecting her own best interests, too. "I'm not trying to force your hand, Jason. I'm just laying things out on the table. So, under the circumstances, I think it's best if I quit working for you. I'm nearly finished with the inventory anyway. So it won't take you—or whoever you get to replace me—long to catch on to my system and complete what I started."

He studied her for a moment, as if he couldn't believe what she was saying.

If truth be told, she found herself wanting to rein in the words, too. But she didn't want to be swept off her feet by a man offering her all the treasures in the world, but none of the promises. She wanted to fall in love with someone who truly felt the same way about her. And how else could she be sure of that?

"I respect your decision," he said. "But will you wait to leave until Braden gets home? I expect him on Monday."

"Sure, I can do that." What would it hurt?

But when Jason walked out of her room, closing both doors between them, her heart ached something fierce.

What would it hurt indeed?

Jason had never been turned down before—not since he was in high school, anyway.

He'd told Juliana that he cared for her, but it was more than that. He wasn't entirely sure how much more, though. Guys like him didn't fall in love.

Hell, he wasn't even sure what kind of a guy he was. Certainly not like his old man. But what if he'd tried so hard to impress his father that he'd become just like him? What if he, too, failed at love and marriage? What if he couldn't love Juliana the way she deserved to be loved?

If he made a commitment to a single mother, he'd be responsible for her baby, too—one way or another. But what if he couldn't provide the kind of loving home and family the child would need? What if he ended up hurting the woman and child he'd come to care about?

That's what concerned Juliana. And that's why she wanted to cut bait now, rather than find out what might happen in the long run.

He probably ought to step back and let her go, but he didn't want to.

Damn. Was this how his father had felt when Camilla left the ranch? If so, it was one hell of a hurt. And one he was going to do his best to ease without compromising himself.

Jason had never cared this much about a woman

in his life. And whether Juliana believed it or not, he wanted more than sex. He wanted to look out for her, to protect her.

He suspected it had something to do with her pregnancy, her vulnerability. But whatever it was, he couldn't help the overwhelming need to make sure she and her baby would be all right. And the only way he could do that was if he kept her close.

That left him in a quandary, though. He wasn't marriage material. He'd never had loving parents to emulate, so what did he know about the kind of work it took to make a long-term relationship last?

Hell, he couldn't even connect with his own brother and sister. So what kind of husband or father would he be?

But he wasn't ready to let Juliana walk out of his life. Not yet.

So he took a seat at the desk in his room, pulled up his contact list and dialed Doug Broderick. After apologizing for calling so late, he said, "Listen, I have a confession to make—and a favor to ask."

"What's that?"

"You remember that change to the artwork I suggested to the marketing department? Well, that idea actually came from an artist who's been helping me at the ranch in Brighton Valley. She's looking for work in the city, and I'd like to offer her a position at Rayburn Enterprises."

"I thought you never got involved with HR decisions," Doug said.

"And I don't actually plan to this time. That's why

I'm calling you. I want you to do it for me—and I don't want her or anyone at the home office to know that I had anything to do with it."

"That's not going to be easy to do."

Jason knew that, but Doug was a spin master. "You'll figure it out. I'll send you her name and number in a text. You can let her know that the marketing department learned that the suggestion came from her. Tell her they were so impressed that they'd like to hire her. Then offer her a full benefit package—a 401(k), health insurance, plus we'll pick up any medical bills that the insurance won't cover. We'll also pay for relocation costs to Houston in a couple weeks, plus a bonus for taking the job."

"That's awfully generous. What kind of experience does she have?"

"Not much, but I'm sure she'll be a great addition to the team."

Doug paused, and Jason had no doubt what he was thinking. But Doug hadn't moved up the ranks as quickly as he had by objecting to a direct order.

"When do you want her to start?" he asked.

"The job will require her to work from the Brighton Valley office for the next few weeks, which is temporarily located at the Leaning R. So once she's finished with the ranch inventory, the marketing team will need to set up some projects she can work on remotely."

"I see."

Did he? Doug might have his suspicions, but he wouldn't know exactly why Jason was so dead set on

keeping Juliana around, even after her job was finished. And maybe it was best that he didn't.

"Just make sure the offer comes from marketing—
and not from me. I don't want to have anything to do
with it. If something doesn't work out, you can be the
one to let her go."

"Okay, boss. It's Friday night, so it's going to take
a while for me to put things into motion so they'll run
smoothly when the news of her hire comes through.
I may not be able to contact her until Monday afternoon."

"That's fine."

Doug chuckled. "I have to say, you handled that just
the way your father would have."

The praise, which might have caused Jason's heart
to soar in the past, left him uneasy. But right now, he
couldn't see any other way around it, short of propos-
ing.

And that was out of the question.

Chapter Ten

The ride back to the ranch was quiet and awkward at first, but thanks to satellite radio, country music soon filled the gaps in conversation.

Jason didn't bring up the discussion they'd had last night, and Juliana was glad. Nor did he press her to continue working for him past Monday, when Braden and Carly were supposed to arrive for the family meeting. She was grateful for that, too. The sooner she moved to Houston, got settled and could finally tell her mother about the baby, the better she was going to feel. And if all went according to plan, she'd be able to reveal her secret and ease her mom's mind about how she'd be able to care for her daughter on her own well before she actually gave birth.

When they finally arrived at the Leaning R, Jason

went to find Ian and check on the teenage boys while Juliana entered the house.

As she surveyed the boxes that lined the far wall of the dining room, she estimated that she had at least two-thirds of the inventory listed and packed. By the time Braden and Carly arrived, her job would be nearly done anyway.

And she'd been right. The next two days passed uneventfully, and on Monday morning, when she entered the kitchen, Jason had fixed breakfast—toast and bacon.

"I'm sorry," he said. "I was going to scramble eggs, but we were out of them. I think I'll send one of the boys into town to pick up supplies. He can get groceries, too, if you want to make a list."

She planned to leave this afternoon—or tomorrow morning, at the latest. But she was probably more familiar with the cooking supplies than he was. At least she knew they were out of eggs and milk. "Sure. Send him in before he leaves."

Jason glanced at her expanding waist and smiled. "The baby must have doubled in size these past three weeks. So I figured you wouldn't want to go into town."

"You're right." She hadn't been able to zip her jeans this morning, let alone button them. And her top was stretched snug across her middle. No way did she want to risk being seen in Brighton Valley. There was no hiding her pregnancy anymore.

Come to think of it, her secret would be out the moment Carly and Braden arrived. She'd have to ask them to keep it to themselves until she had a chance to tell her mom.

"What time do you expect your brother and sister?" she asked.

"Carly said she'd be here around two, although Braden will probably get here sooner."

"Okay. I'll be sure to put on a pot of coffee."

"Maybe we should add a dozen doughnuts to that shopping list. It might sweeten everyone's mood."

"Maybe…" But suddenly, Juliana had a better idea. She'd go through Granny's recipe box and bake something special. Maybe it would help them remember their roots and feel like the family they were meant to be.

There she went again, trying to fix the Rayburns. But then again, Jason had done a lot for her. The least she could do was to try and pay him back the only way she could.

Well, at least it would keep her mind off Camilla and that romantic mystery.

Jason moved closer and cupped her cheek—the first intimate gesture he'd made since Friday night. She'd missed his touch, more than she cared to let on. Yet in spite of any hesitation she might have had, she placed her hand over his, holding their momentary bond.

Then, realizing she might be sending mixed messages, she released him.

He didn't object. Instead, he stepped aside, reached in the cabinet under the sink for the dish soap, then turned on the faucet.

Odd, she thought. After Friday night, she would

have expected things between them to be awkward, but they weren't. Jason seemed to accept her reason for turning him down, which she found more than a little surprising. She would have thought he might resent her.

He seemed to care about her, though. Did he expect her to change her mind?

Then again, maybe he was more thoughtful and understanding than she'd realized.

"Go on outside," she said. "You fixed breakfast, so I'll do the cleanup."

"Thanks." He tossed her a grin, then headed for the mudroom, where he'd left his boots and his hat.

As she watched the CEO morph into a rancher, albeit a temporary one, she couldn't help but admire his masculine form as well as his work ethic. Would it be wrong to reconsider, to see where a relationship with him might go?

Had that been part of his game plan all along?

Oh, for Pete's sake. Look at how skeptical Alex had made her. Jason had been nothing but a gentleman since she'd met him.

When the back door shut, she snatched a piece of bacon from the plate on the counter and popped it in her mouth.

While the sink filled with warm, soapy water, she pulled out Granny's recipe box from the cupboard. She loved reading the notes written on the back of each card. She would choose a good recipe—something clearly marked as a family favorite—to make today, then check the pantry to see what ingredients she'd need to add to the shopping list.

In the meantime, she glanced out the kitchen window and spotted Jason in the yard.

Maybe she shouldn't have turned him down while they'd been in San Antonio. Maybe she should apologize for not taking him at his word.

And see if he might consider going slow—and giving her another chance.

In spite of what Jason had said, Carly arrived at the ranch before Braden and just after one thirty.

Juliana greeted her in the living room. But when she approached her friend for a hug, Carly put up her hands to stop her from getting too close.

"I feel fine today," Carly said, "so I don't think I'm contagious. But just in case, you better not get near me. I've been sick the past couple of evenings. In the morning, when I wake up, I feel much better. But then at work, it hits me again. I must be pushing myself too hard. Hopefully, with two days off, I can get some rest and kick that bug once and for all."

"I hope so," Juliana said. "I'm sure they don't want you calling in sick too often."

"That's true. They'll let me go and keep my understudy instead." Carly plopped down on the sofa, then glanced at Juliana, her gaze landing on her waistline. "Oh, wow. Look at you."

Juliana placed a hand on her baby bump. "Now you can see why that breakup with Alex was especially unsettling."

"I can't believe he was married and never told you. What a jerk. Does your mom know?"

"Not yet. I don't have the heart to tell her."

"You can't keep your pregnancy a secret forever."

"I don't intend to. I just want to get settled in Houston first. I hope to be able to tell her within the next couple of weeks."

"In person?"

Juliana's cheeks warmed, and she took a seat on the sofa next to Carly. "No, I'll probably do it over the phone. That way I won't have to worry about any of her neighbors seeing me. She can decide when and what she wants to tell them herself. But after I spill the beans, I'll invite her and Gram over for lunch and let them see for themselves that I'm doing fine."

Carly didn't say anything.

"What's the matter?" Juliana asked. "Do you think I'm wrong for not telling her face to face?"

"I'm the last one in the world to point fingers at you. I was seeing a guy recently, and ever since we broke up, I've been avoiding him, too."

"Who is he?"

Carly glanced around the room. After seeing they were alone, she still lowered her voice. "Ian. But don't tell Jason."

"Why not?"

"Because Ian wanted me to live on the ranch and oversee it for the family, but I can't do that and have a career, too. And if Jason knew, he'd pressure me to do the same thing. He can be pretty persuasive when he puts his mind to something. He's like my dad was in that sense, and I'm not going to let him talk me into doing something I don't want to do."

That didn't sound like the man Juliana had gotten to know. "Do you really think Jason would try to force your hand?"

"He's done it before."

At least he hadn't tried to pressure Juliana into having an affair with him. Or to continue working for him longer than she thought was wise. He'd been respectful of her feelings. That had to count for something, didn't it?

She glanced at the boxes she'd packed. "By the way, Ralph Nettles came by and took a look at the ranch. He doesn't think it will take very long to sell. He might even have a buyer who's interested."

"I guess that's good news," Carly said. "I hate to see strangers take over, but not at the expense of my happiness. I've had to live in my parents' shadows all my life, and it's time I did something on my own."

Juliana took her friend's hand. "I understand. Just know that I'm in your corner."

Carly gave her fingers a warm squeeze. "And I'll always be in yours."

At the sound of a vehicle pulling up in the drive, both women got up and looked out the window.

"Braden's here," Juliana said. And Jason was greeting him in the yard. "I'd better put on the coffee."

By the time Jason and his rugged, blond-haired brother entered the living room, the coffee gurgled in the pot and the fresh-brewed aroma filled the air.

Some might consider her tricky, but Juliana didn't care. She'd done her best to create a nostalgic mood by placing Granny's best cups and saucers on the table.

She'd unpacked them earlier today. She would have to wash and repack them after everyone left, but she wanted the siblings to be reminded of their childhood and the woman they'd all loved.

Then she sliced large pieces of the Texas chocolate cake she'd baked. "A real kid-pleaser," Granny had written on the back of the recipe card. "It'll take the fire out of the feistiest old coot."

Just what she needed. Something the kids had loved—and a peace offering, just in case someone wanted to put up a fuss.

Next she filled the creamer and sugar bowl. When she'd set the table, she went out and called the Rayburns to the antique mahogany table in the dining room, where they'd undoubtedly shared many a meal with Granny.

As Carly and Braden each grabbed a chair, Juliana was about to excuse herself, but Jason stopped her. "We can discuss family business later. I'd like to talk about Dad and Camilla first. So why don't you stick around?"

She glanced at Carly, and then at Braden, who both nodded. So she took a seat.

When Carly glanced down at her plate, her breath caught. "Oh, my gosh. Is this Texas chocolate cake?"

"I found Granny's recipe box," Juliana admitted. "And I thought I'd try some of her favorites. I had a little sliver while I was in the kitchen, and I decided it was a great choice. What do you think?"

"This was always my favorite," Carly said as she grabbed her fork. "I was afraid I'd never get to have it again."

"She's right," Braden added. "This is awesome. Would you give me that recipe card, Juliana?"

At his brother's surprising question, Jason leaned forward. "You bake?"

"I've been known to on occasion. Why?"

"No reason." Just that there was another thing he didn't know about his brother. "But I have to tell you, when Juliana found that recipe box, it was a real coup. She's surprised me a couple of times with some of my favorite meals."

Braden winked at her. "Jules is one of a kind."

Jules? So he had a nickname for her. And Jason's nickname had been Bird Legs. Boy, had he missed the mark. She was a jewel, all right.

"So tell me what you know already," Braden said.

"Camilla Cruz was Reuben Montoya's daughter," Jason said. "Dad probably met her here at the ranch and fell for her. But she broke things off and left him."

"She must have stayed here within the past few years," Juliana added, "because there's a portrait of Granny in the bedroom that Camilla painted. And Granny's wearing one of her newer dresses."

"No kidding? I've never seen it." Braden looked at Carly. "Have you?"

"Yes, but I didn't think anything of it. I just figured Granny must have commissioned someone to paint it." Carly bit down on her bottom lip and furrowed her brow. Then she looked at Jason. "But if Camilla was the daughter of the old Leaning R foreman, why did she and Reuben have different last names?"

"Maybe she was married," Jason said. "Or she might have wanted a professional name."

"How did you know that Dad was in love with her?" Braden asked. "That seems like quite a stretch. I'd be more inclined to think that he was obsessed with her because she wasn't interested in him."

Jason told him about the love letter they'd found, about the storage shed, the artwork.

"That puts a different spin on it," Braden said.

Jason leaned forward. "What do you mean?"

"I wasn't aware of the import business. But Dad was looking for her and Reuben when he was in Mexico."

"That's what I don't understand. He even hired a private investigator, but a simple internet search would have told him that Camilla died of breast cancer last year in San Diego."

"That's what I wanted to know. It seems that Reuben's sister was also named Camilla. That might have been the woman Dad was looking for."

"If Camilla, the woman he supposedly loved, was gone, why would Dad go in search of her father and her aunt?"

"Because Camilla had two young children, and Reuben had been looking after them while she went to San Diego for her treatment. And when Reuben passed about four months ago, I think the children were sent to an orphanage. I might be wrong, but my gut tells me that's who Dad was looking for."

"Camilla's kids?" That was certainly possible. "Did he find them?"

"No, but you know how Dad felt about child support and charities that benefited kids—even if he didn't have time to spend with his own. I don't think he wanted Camilla's children to be abandoned to an orphanage."

"So why did you continue Dad's search?" Jason asked.

Braden shrugged. "It's hard to explain. I guess if it was that important to Dad, someone ought to follow through for him. But then my mom called and told me that my grandpa isn't expected to live, so I need to be here for him—and for her."

"Of course," Jason said.

"Do you think Camilla's kids could be the children in that portrait we found in the storage unit?" Juliana asked.

"Who knows?" Jason looked at his brother. "What did you find out about the kids?"

"From what I learned, they're twins—a boy and a girl. I think they'd be about six or seven years old."

Jason's stomach clenched. And after losing both their mother and grandfather, they'd been taken from the only home they knew, the only family they had? Poor kids.

In spite of his obligations at the corporate headquarters, Jason felt compelled to continue the search, although he wasn't sure why.

For Braden? For their father?

Or maybe just for the brother and sister stuck in an orphanage.

It seemed like the right thing to do, even if it wasn't his obligation.

How weird was that?

But somehow, it had become a family quest. And something he was determined to pursue, even if he had to hire the private-investigating firm to continue the search.

The meeting to discuss the sale of the ranch and the division of the heirlooms and furniture seemed to have gone fairly well. At least, Jason shook Braden's hand when it ended. And they all went out to the yard, where Braden got into his pickup.

"Let me know if there's anything I can do for you or your mother," Jason said. "I mean it."

Braden nodded.

Carly climbed into her own car, intending to follow Braden back to his ranch, where she would visit his mom and spend the night. After they both drove off, Jason went out to the barn, leaving Juliana to return to the house.

After she washed, dried and repacked the dishes they'd used earlier, she resealed the box. As she straightened, she again studied the work she'd already completed. She'd told Jason she would leave as soon as the family meeting was over, so she was free to pack and head out.

But did she really want to leave?

What would it hurt to stick it out until the house was completely packed? After all, she'd made a commitment.

She'd also suggested that she wanted one from

him—and after only three weeks. Had that been entirely fair?

Not really. Maybe she should lie down for a while and give it some serious thought.

She'd just returned to the bedroom when her cell phone rang. She didn't recognize the number, but she was glad to see it wasn't Alex trying to contact her again.

"Is this Juliana Bailey?" the male caller asked.

"Yes, it is."

"This is Douglas Broderick of Rayburn Enterprises."

The call took her aback. "What can I do for you?"

"That was a great suggestion you made for the art layout. It made all the difference in the world to the promotional campaign, and the marketing department was very impressed."

She straightened and smiled. "I'm glad I could help, Mr. Broderick."

"So are we. And as a result, we think you'd make a fine addition to Rayburn Enterprises. We're willing to offer you a very generous benefit package, including a 401(k), health insurance, plus we'll pick up any medical bills that the insurance won't cover. We'll also pay for relocation costs to Houston in a couple weeks, plus a bonus for taking the job." He then quoted a starting salary that more than stunned her.

Whoa. Had he said *generous*? The offer was much more than that. It was…mind-boggling. And way over the top. Which made her more than a little suspicious…

"Did Jason Rayburn have anything to do with this?" she asked.

"No, Mr. Rayburn makes it a firm rule not to get involved in any HR decisions. He did, however, mention that you were the person responsible for solving our marketing dilemma. He also gave me your phone number. But the decision to hire you was mine alone."

Without an interview or a background check? And not even a drug test?

"We've needed some new blood and some fresh ideas on our team," he added. "And we believe you're the spark that will put the art department back on track."

While the offer was indeed flattering, it was also a bit unsettling.

"We realize that you're committed to finishing a job, but that's not a problem. We actually have several projects you can handle for us from the remote office Mr. Rayburn has set up in Brighton Valley until your new office is ready for you in Houston."

Seriously? And Jason knew very little about this? Her BS meter was shooting off the charts.

"Can I have some time to think about it?" she asked.

Mr. Broderick paused a beat. "Um, yes. Of course. How much time do you think you'll need?"

"A day or so."

After he gave her the number to his direct line, she ended the call.

You'd think she'd be on top of the world. The offer was way more than she'd ever dreamed of earning. And it would solve all her problems. She'd be able to relocate to Houston, hire a competent nanny and provide well for her baby. But that's what she found so bothersome.

Why would a corporation offer a woman with virtually no experience in the field and only an AA degree a position with a salary and a benefit package like that?

Something wasn't right. And as badly as she needed the job and the money, as flattering and as tempting as the offer had been, she couldn't jump on it. Not without doing a bit of research.

So she used her smartphone, accessed the internet and checked out the employment opportunities at Rayburn Enterprises, as well as the job requirements and the salaries.

It didn't take long for her suspicion to prove true. New hires with only an AA degree weren't given salaries and benefit packages like she'd been offered.

In spite of what Mr. Broderick had told her, Jason had to have had something to do with that call.

Was he trying to manipulate her? He had to be. He was holding that job out to her like a carrot, tempting her to be his lover.

But not his wife.

Like Alex, he wanted her at his beck and call—on his terms, but not on her own.

Well, fool me once, shame on you. Fool me twice, shame on me.

And Juliana was nobody's fool.

Chapter Eleven

After paying the delivery man from Romano's Pizzeria, who'd brought a medium pepperoni and a small vegetarian as well as an antipasto salad, Jason set the table out on the back porch. He figured that would be the best place to have dinner tonight.

He and Juliana had a lot to talk about—and not just the family meeting he'd had with Carly and Braden.

Juliana had disappeared after his brother and sister left, but Doug had said he'd call and make that job offer sometime this afternoon. It was already after five, so she was probably in her room, pondering her good news and making plans for her move.

When she broached the subject, he'd confirm that he never got involved with HR decisions, so he'd had nothing to do with the offer. But he'd admit that he was happy for her—and that he looked forward to having her join the firm.

In most cases—at least 99 percent of them—he considered honesty the best policy. But for now, he'd prefer to let Juliana think the offer had come through because of her own merits. And, in a way, it really had. She'd proven herself to be the kind of woman he wanted to work with—and to be with. So who knew where that might lead?

His father had needed to prove himself to Camilla, but the only person Jason had anything to prove to was himself, because he wasn't sure what kind of man he really was. Or what kind of husband or father he might make. Only time would tell, he supposed.

He glanced at his watch. Juliana had probably received the call from Doug by now, and he couldn't wait to hear what she had to say. He'd feign surprise, of course.

But when she walked outside, carrying her suitcase and her purse, he didn't have a chance to fake his surprise.

"What are you doing?" he asked.

"I'm leaving."

Had Doug screwed up and forgotten that Juliana was to stay here and move to Houston when Jason's time in Brighton Valley was through? Doug usually took notes when Jason gave him an assignment. Either way, Doug would have to tell her there'd been a change in plans or something.

"Where are you going?" Jason asked.

"I'm not sure."

Uh-oh. That didn't seem right. And neither did the cool glare in her eyes. If the call from Doug had come through, she should be happy. "What's wrong?"

She dropped her bag on the ground, crossed her arms and shifted her weight to one hip. "Did you have anything to do with that job Rayburn Enterprises just offered me?"

He'd planned to deny it, but something obviously had gone south, and the only way to rectify the situation was to confess. "Actually, I did. I thought if it came through the proper channels, you might be more apt to agree."

"Then you thought wrong. I'm not going to accept it. In fact, I'm finished here. I quit."

Her words struck him like an undercut to the jaw, and he struggled to catch his breath, let alone speak. "I… I don't understand."

"After everything we've talked about, everything you've learned about me… Jason, what kind of a person do you think I am?"

He thought she was a wonderful woman who'd found herself in a tough situation, and he was trying to help her out. He was offering her a hell of a lot more than she could get job hunting on her own—and not as a charity case. It was because…he cared for her. But she wasn't going to force him to say something he wasn't sure he felt. Something he wasn't sure he was even able to feel.

"I was just trying to help. Did you find that offensive in some way?"

"Help me? Is that what you were trying to do? Or were you trying to buy my affection?"

"You're wrong," he said. "I care for you, but I can't give you what you want. I can, however, give you what you need."

Her frown deepened, and she stooped to pick up her bag. "How in the world would you know that? You aren't even aware of what *you* need." Then she started toward her car.

"What about the money you've earned so far?" he asked.

She continued to walk without turning around. "Give it to Carly. I'll get it from her."

So she wasn't even going to give him a forwarding address? She'd done the same thing when she'd left La Galleria, just faded into obscurity.

"You're a great one for running away from your problems," he said.

At that she did turn. "Don't you dare point out my flaws and shortcomings when you refuse to even consider that you might have any at all. But just for the record, Mr. Rayburn, you have plenty."

Then she opened the car door, tossed in her bag and climbed behind the wheel.

She was barreling down the graveled driveway and kicking up rocks and dust before he could acknowledge that she was right.

Never had he felt so alone in his life—or so much like his father. However, Charles Rayburn had always considered himself a success in all things—women, fame and fortune.

Yet tonight, Jason felt anything but.

For the first mile, Juliana wasn't sure where she was going. And by the time she'd passed the second, the tears welling in her eyes made it difficult to even see the road.

She was two for two when it came to choosing men. What was her problem? Was she wearing some kind of neon sign that flashed *Naive Lover*? *Kept Woman*?

Well, Jason had read her wrong. She could—and would—provide a home for herself and the baby. It might not be anything flashy, but she wouldn't compromise her integrity with a corporate position and salary she hadn't earned.

Ooh. She could throttle him. She'd never been prone to violence, but if he were sitting next to her, she'd throw something at him, although she didn't know what. Her purse was the only thing handy.

"Damn you, Jason Rayburn!"

Yet as her car continued to roll along the country road, she realized he'd had a point. She hadn't wanted to confront her problems, at least when it came to talking to her mother.

Sure, she'd been avoiding the discussion because she didn't want her mom to feel any more embarrassed or hurt than necessary. But in truth, it was more than that. Juliana hadn't wanted to see the look of disappointment on her mom's face, either.

But she was going to see that same expression

whether she waited a week or four more months to tell her. Dragging it on was just causing her unnecessary stress. She might as well get it over with. Besides, she wasn't ever going to be happy until she quit running away from her mistake with Alex and faced it head-on.

So instead of turning onto the interstate that would take her to Houston, she headed to downtown Brighton Valley. Her mom and grandmother would be home having dinner now, which would be the perfect time to tell them both.

Ten minutes later, she parked behind the drugstore, where her mom and grandmother shared the two-bedroom apartment upstairs. She left her bag locked in the trunk, although she might ask if she could spend the night on their sofa bed and drive to the city in the morning. Then she climbed the back stairs to the entrance.

She rapped lightly on the door, and Gram greeted her with a smile. "Julie, what a nice surprise. Come in, you're just in time for dinner. We're having meat loaf and baked potato. Are you hungry?"

"I could eat a little something, if you have enough."

"We have plenty," Gram said as she turned away from Juliana and returned to the small kitchen area.

The two-bedroom apartment was just as she remembered—small, but cozy and clean. The living area opened up to the kitchen, so it was easy to see that dinner was ready.

"Let me set out a plate for you," Gram said, while facing the cupboard. "Your mom is changing out of her work clothes. She'll be out in a minute."

Juliana took a seat at the dinette table, which hid her tummy, and watched as Gram set out a third place setting.

Gram had already shed her business clothes and slipped into a turquoise Hawaiian muumuu. "We've missed having you here, honey. How's the temporary job going?"

Juliana rested her elbows on the table. "It went well, but it's over."

"That's too bad. What's next?"

"Why don't I tell you and Mom together? That's actually why I came. There's something I should have talked you about a few months ago."

"Sounds like bad news."

"Well, I guess that depends on how you look at it. I'd call it good news." Juliana hoped her mother would feel the same way, once she got over the initial shock and disappointment.

The bedroom door swung open, and her mother stepped out wearing a floral blouse and white shorts. She brightened when she saw Juliana. "I thought I heard your voice. Why didn't you call and let us know you were coming? We would have picked up some ice cream or something sweet to have for dessert."

"Actually, I came to make a confession and to share my news."

"Don't tell me," Mom said. "You applied for a job in the city and got it. I knew that was coming. I've been praying you'd find something close, but I guess that wasn't meant to be."

"Is that your confession?" Gram asked, a gray brow

arched, indicating she thought there might be more to it than that.

Juliana took a deep breath, then proceeded to tell them about Alex Montgomery, his lies and how she'd mistakenly gotten involved with him. "And that's the real reason I quit working at the art gallery. I didn't want to be around him anymore. He actually had the gall to think I'd be interested in continuing our relationship—on the sly, of course."

"Why, that ornery rascal," Grandma said. "Shame on him. I don't have any respect for a lying cheater."

"I agree," Juliana said. "But there's more to the story." A *lot* more. She got to her feet and placed her hand on her baby bump. She didn't have to say anything more. Both women could clearly see the part she hadn't mentioned.

"Oh, my," her mother said as tears filled her eyes.

Gram clicked her tongue. "Does the scoundrel know?"

"Yes and no. I told him I was pregnant, which is when he decided to confess that he was married. He asked me to get rid of it."

"Humph." Gram crossed her arms.

"I'm glad you're having the baby," Mom said.

Juliana turned to her, lips parted. "You are? I was afraid you'd be…upset or embarrassed. I mean, you work at the church. What are people going to think if your unwed daughter ran off and got pregnant by a married man?"

"First off," Mom said, "no one needs to know any details. It's none of their business. And second, the folks at church are supposed to be in the business of forgiveness and turning the other cheek. They'll just have to learn to practice what they preach, honey."

Juliana stared at her mother, who was smiling in spite of wiping the tears from her eyes. "Seriously? You're not upset?"

"Well, to be honest, I'm as mad as a wet hen at that man—Mr. Montgomery, I assume? And I'd like to wring his neck." She shook her head. "I'm also heart-broken to think you were betrayed and hurt. It won't be easy to raise a child on your own, but I admire you for it. Babies are a blessing, Julie. I know you'll be a wonderful mama, and Gram and I are here to help you. So what's there for me to be upset about?"

"Well, *I'm* plenty stirred up," Gram said. "What's that fella's name again? I'd like to drive into Wexler and give him a piece of my mind."

No doubt she would, given the chance. Gram was a feisty one. She bowled on Tuesday nights with the American Legion and played softball on the weekends with the Hot Mamas, a league of women, most of whom were twenty or more years her junior. She even kept a Louisville Slugger by the front door to ward off in-truders. Of course, that was because Sheriff Hollister had confiscated her pistol last spring when she had a nightmare and fired several shots out the window and into Main Street.

Juliana smiled and gave Gram a hug. "Please don't do that. Haven't you ever heard the old phrase *let sleep-ing dogs lie*?"

"Hmm," Mom said. "Maybe we should say, 'Let

lying rats sleep.' Either way, I want to know more about my new grandbaby. Do you know what you're having?"

"A little girl," Juliana said.

Mom leaned back and clapped her hands together. "She'll be a winter baby, so I can start knitting blankets and booties." She turned to Grandma. "Won't this be fun, Mother? We have some shopping to do."

It would be fun at that. As the two women began to make plans and discuss baby names, Juliana sat back and marveled at the reception her news had gotten. Maybe she wouldn't need to find a job in Houston after all, which was just as well, she supposed.

The only thing she wouldn't confess was the experience she'd had with Jason. But why tell them about him?

Nothing would become of it. She'd made sure of it when she turned down his job offer and left him standing on the porch, staring at her in disbelief.

Jason had no idea how long he'd stood outside last night, wondering what in the world to do about Juliana. Now that he'd met her, now that she'd shared a small part of his life, he couldn't seem to get her out of his mind.

She'd bewitched him or something. Whatever it was, nothing else seemed to matter other than making things right between them.

But he had no idea how or where to start. He'd certainly botched things up when he'd tried to hire her.

After finally turning in, he'd slept like hell and

woken up early. But still he'd yet to come up with a solution.

It wasn't until he went into Granny's kitchen, poured himself a cup of coffee and cut a slice of leftover Texas chocolate cake that things began to make sense.

For some reason, as he studied the pale blue floral print on the coffee mug and savored that familiar sweet dessert, he could almost hear that sweet old woman pointing him in the right direction, as she'd done so many times when he'd been a boy she'd lovingly nick-named Jay-Ray.

Life isn't all about money. It's about love and family. Nothing matters until you're willing to put your heart on the line.

Was he willing to do that with Juliana?

His father never had been able to put anyone ahead of his pursuit of financial success. And even though Jason had struggled hard to be his own man, he feared there was just a little too much of Charles in him to be any different.

Could he be the kind of husband and father Juliana and her baby needed?

He thought of her again, remembered her leaning against the doorjamb in the office, stroking the gentle swell of her womb and talking about her baby and its father. *I'm going to teach her to be honest and loving and kind. So even if she ends up looking like her dad, she won't be anything like him.*

Jason's mother had died early, so who'd taught him to be different from his old man?

Granny had tried, but he feared he'd failed her like his father had.

You're a good boy, Jay-Ray. You know right from wrong, so you won't disappoint me like your daddy did.

Would she be disappointed in the man he'd become?

It seemed that everyone thought he'd followed in his dad's footsteps. *You handled that just the way your father would have*, Doug had said.

He supposed he had, but that hadn't been his intent. And his conscience was kicking in, telling him to take corrective action. Didn't that mean something?

I judge a man by his character, the feed-store owner had said, *not his bloodlines.*

Maybe it was time for Jason's true character to step up to the plate and for him to lay his heart on the line, no matter what.

Wasn't Juliana worth the risk?

Early the next morning, Jason drove to town. He wasn't sure if Juliana would be at her mother's apartment, but that's where he'd start his search.

When he pulled into the alley behind the drugstore and spotted her car, he parked beside it. Then he climbed the back stairs and knocked at the door.

A woman wearing a blue robe and pink spongy curlers in her silver hair answered. He assumed she was the grandmother.

"Can I help you?" she asked.

"Yes, ma'am. I'm looking for Juliana Bailey."

The elderly woman stiffened. "Julie's in the shower, but she doesn't want to talk to you."

"I understand. And I don't blame her for being upset, but I'd like to apologize—"

The woman lifted a baseball bat that been resting by the door and shook it at him. "Do I need to run you out of here? I have no tolerance for liars."

What in the hell had Juliana told her family about him? He hadn't lied to her. Maybe he'd neglected to tell her the whole truth, but—

At that, another woman—Juliana's mom?—came out of the bedroom wearing a floral robe. "Who is it, Mother?"

"It's that louse who hurt our little girl, and I'm going to knock his head right out of the ballpark if he doesn't get off our stoop."

"You're trespassing," Mrs. Bailey said as she snatched the telephone from its cradle. "If you don't leave right this minute, I'm going to call the sheriff and have you arrested."

Jason had no idea how he could have hurt Juliana this badly. Her mom wanted to have him arrested, and her grandmother wanted to kill him. Didn't this prove that he wasn't any good at relationships?

Yet he didn't want to leave without getting a chance to talk to Juliana personally.

Maybe it would be in his best interest if Sheriff Hollister did come and sort all this out. He was just about to suggest it when Juliana entered the fracas.

"Mom? Grandma? What are you doing?" she asked.

"You told this good-for-nothing rascal to leave you and the baby alone, but he didn't listen," the bat-wielding grandmother shouted. "So I'm going to run him off for good."

"Mother," Mrs. Bailey said as she grabbed the older woman's wrist, "don't hit him with that baseball bat. You'll get arrested for assault, and then look at the trouble you'll be in. Just because you work at city hall doesn't mean you have diplomatic immunity."

"No, but I do have some pull."

"Enough," Juliana's mother said, wrenching the bat from her mother's hands. "I'm calling Sheriff Hollister. We'll file a restraining order against Mr. Montgomery, and he won't be able to bother Juliana again."

Montgomery? So *that's* why they'd called Jason a lying cheat and were so all-fired intent upon running him off. He couldn't say that he blamed them, considering the mistaken identity. "You've got this all wrong. Let me explain."

"No," Juliana said. "Let me. He's not the baby's father."

At that, Grandma's scowl vanished, and she turned to Jason sheepishly. "Then who are you?"

"He's Jason Rayburn," Juliana answered. "My former boss."

"Well, you should have said something sooner," Grandma said. "I could have killed you. I have a batting average of three-ninety in the Hot Mamas League."

Jason offered her a smile and tried to make light of the mistake. "If I'd known that and thought you would have swung, I would have hightailed it out of here."

"Maybe you still should." Juliana crossed her arms.

"Sheriff Hollister knows he'd better hurry over here when Gram thinks she has a prowler."

Apparently, he'd only eased the imminent threat of violence. "Juliana, if you don't mind, I need to talk to you. I'd like to apologize."

"Come on in," Grandma said. "We'd like to hear what you have to say."

We? Surely Juliana would ask for privacy. Wouldn't she?

When all three women stepped aside, he realized he was going to have an audience.

All right then. If that's the way she wanted it… "I'm sorry for offering you the job in Houston. I was wrong for beating around the bush. I should have been more direct, but I was afraid."

"Of what?" Juliana asked. "Having to fire me when you grew tired of having me around?"

When Grandma eased toward Mrs. Bailey, who held the bat, Jason beat her to it, snatching the weapon from Juliana's mother. "I'm sorry, ladies, but I'd feel a lot better if I could hold on to this for a while. Feel free to call the sheriff, though."

He tossed Juliana a smile, but she didn't return it. Okay, then. He'd better get back to the apology. "I was insensitive and selfish, and I'm sorry. I was afraid to admit how I was feeling about you. Over the past few weeks, I fell in love with you, but it scared the crap out of me. I've never felt this way before, and I'm not sure what to do with it. I haven't seen an example of a successful marriage or even a long-lasting relationship before, and what if I suck at it? What if I fail you? I'd not only hurt you, but I'd risk hurting the baby, too."

"You love me?" Juliana asked, her voice softening along with her stance.

"Doesn't that scare you?" he asked.

"Actually, it makes me feel a whole lot better about loving you."

She loved him, too?

"So I'm not alone in this?" he asked.

"No, you're not. And just so you know, I'm not sure what to make of it all, either. It happened so fast. But I *do* love you, Jason Rayburn."

"All right," he said, "then I'd like to apply for a job. And I'm willing to give you my résumé, which is sadly lacking in experience and education. But I'm eager to learn."

"What job is that?"

"I might not be your baby's biological father," Jason said, "but I'd like to apply for the daddy position—if it's available."

Tears welled in her eyes, and her lips quivered as they formed a smile. "The job is definitely open."

"How about the position of husband? I'm afraid I'm lacking in that department, too."

Her eyes widened, and her lips parted. "You want to marry me?"

"I didn't buy a ring yet, which I think was probably my first mistake in Bridegroom 101. So you can see that I have a lot to learn."

Juliana laughed while swiping at the tears streaming down her cheeks. "I don't need a ring."

"Oh, yes, she does," Grandma said. "It doesn't have to be a diamond, but a band of some kind is expected."

Juliana kissed her grandmother. "I know you mean well, and I love you to pieces. But I think it's time Jason and I discussed the rest of these details on our own."

Jason handed the bat to Grandma, trusting she wouldn't use it on him anymore. Then he took Juliana in his arms, burying his face in her hair, savoring her exotic scent and the feel of her in his arms. "I love you, Juliana. We'll work it all out one way or another."

Then he kissed her with all the love in his heart, a silent promise to do whatever it took to be the best husband and father he could, for now and for always.

When the kiss ended, the audience of two broke into smiles, clearly pleased by what had unfolded.

"I'd rather not have a long engagement," he told Juliana. "Unless you want one."

"Are you sure?" she asked.

"I'm more sure with every minute I stand here. So what do you say?"

"Yes, I'll marry you."

At that, cheers broke out.

"Jason," Mrs. Bailey said, "let me be the first to welcome you to the family. Some of us might be a little wild and woolly, especially if we have a pistol or a baseball bat in hand, but we're also very warm, loving and supportive."

"That is," Grandma said, "as long as you're good to our girls—both of them."

"I promise to do my best," he said. And he meant that from the bottom of his heart.

He drew Juliana close. As Granny had said, life was about love and family. And on that, he was willing to lay his heart.

Chapter Twelve

Less than a week after Jason proposed, Juliana stood in front of a floor-length mirror in the choir room at the Brighton Valley Community Church, adjusting her bridal veil.

The past few days had passed in a happy blur, but everything seemed to fall right into place as if they'd planned their small wedding months in advance. Her dress was a simple white satin gown with an empire waist that she'd found in a shop in Wexler. It fit perfectly and hadn't needed a single alteration.

Wanda at Valley Florists played softball with Gram and had given them a deal on the brightly colored flowers—pincushion proteas, peonies and garden roses.

Her mother stood beside her wearing a pale blue

dress, her brown hair pulled up in a twist. "You look beautiful, honey. But then again, I always knew you would be a beautiful bride someday."

Juliana felt beautiful, probably because she also felt loved and cherished. She glanced at her left hand, where Jason had placed a two-carat diamond just five days ago and where he would soon add a matching band.

She'd never been so happy.

"I'm going to make sure everyone is here and seated," Mom said. "Then I'll let Reverend Steuben know that we're ready to begin."

As her mother slipped out of the room, Juliana turned to her maid of honor and soon-to-be sister-in-law. Carly had driven in from San Antonio this morning and had just finished dressing in a light green sundress she'd purchased recently, but hadn't worn. "Thanks for making the trip on such short notice. I know it wasn't easy for you to get the time off."

Carly smiled, her eyes glimmering. "Actually, it wasn't so tough to get away. They let me go yesterday."

Juliana gasped. "I'm so sorry. What happened?"

"It's that stupid flu bug. I can't seem to kick it. One night I'm fine, then the next, I'm sick as a dog. There's no rhyme or reason for it, but the director said that if he couldn't count on me to be one hundred percent for every performance, he had to cut me loose. So here I am."

"I feel guilty for being so happy when your whole world must be falling apart."

Carly grabbed her hand and gave it a squeeze.

"Don't you dare feel sorry for me today. There'll be other singing gigs."

"Are you feeling better now?" Juliana asked.

"I'm fine. Just tired. But I got up early and drove six hours. I just need to get some rest, which I intend to do tonight. But if that doesn't help, I'll see my doctor while I'm in town."

"That might be a good idea. You don't want to take any chances."

"I won't. By the way, do you think Jason would mind if I stayed at the ranch for a while? I let my apartment in town go when I moved to San Antonio."

"Of course he won't mind. We'll be gone on our honeymoon for a week anyway."

Carly glanced in the mirror and fussed with an errant blond curl. "Where are you going?"

"We're spending the night in Houston, then flying to Guadalajara tomorrow morning."

"Why Mexico…?" Carly straightened and turned away from the mirror. "Wait, don't tell me. Jason plans to take over that search for Braden and look for Camilla's kids."

Juliana nodded. "He's determined to check out some of the orphanages and see if he can find them. He wants to make sure they're okay, and I can't blame him."

"What will you do if you find them?"

"He and Braden have been discussing options."

Carly crossed her arms. "That's interesting. And so is the fact that Jason asked Braden to be his best man today."

Juliana laughed. "It's not like they've become best friends yet."

"Still, it's a start."

Yes, it was. And if Juliana had her way, the brothers would grow closer as time went by.

The door opened, and Juliana's mother poked her head inside. "Everyone's here, Julie. Are you girls ready?"

Juliana adjusted her veil one last time. "Yes, we are."

And with that, she swept out of the choir room, ready to marry the man she loved.

While Jason waited with his brother in the church breezeway, ready to walk through the side door along the altar to stand with the minister who would perform the ceremony, his cell phone rang.

"Are you going to answer that *now*?" Braden asked.

Jason glanced at the display, noting that it was Doug at the home office. "This is the last call I'll take. Then I'll power down—or at least, silence it—for the next few days." He swept his finger across the screen. "Hey, Doug. What's up?"

"Stan Wainwright's attorney called again. How do you want me to respond regarding their proposal?"

"Schedule a meeting for the end of next week. I'm getting married today and will be off the radar for the next four or five days."

"That's a surprise. Who's the lucky woman? Have I met her?"

"No, not yet. It's Juliana Bailey."

"The woman you wanted to hire?"

Jason grinned. "Yep, that's the one."

"She turned down the offer I gave her. Did she change her mind about coming to work for us?"

"No, she'll probably enroll at one of the universities instead. She's still thinking about what she wants to do."

Doug blew out a whistle. "Marriage, huh? I never saw that coming. It sure happened quickly. What'd you decide to do? Elope?"

"Pretty much. It's a small guest list—just family and a few close friends."

Counting the bridal party of four, Braden's mom and Juliana's mother and grandmother, the family members only numbered seven. But even with the few friends Karen Bailey and Gram had invited, the church was going to be nearly empty.

Of course, Jason had brought the portrait of Granny and placed it in the front row. It only seemed right that she be there in spirit, although he sensed she would be looking down on them anyway.

"Well, boss," Doug said, "I wish you and your new wife all the best. I'm looking forward to meeting her."

"Thanks, I appreciate that. We'll stop by the office when we get back from our honeymoon."

After disconnecting the line and shutting off the power, Jason turned to Braden. "I won't turn it back on until I call you from Guadalajara."

"What's your first step going to be after you find the kids?" Braden asked.

"I'll look for Camilla's next of kin—or someone who'll provide them with a good home."

"And what if there isn't anyone? Dad wouldn't have left them in an orphanage."

"You're right. So if that's the case, then you and I will have to put our heads together and come up with a solution. Maybe someone in Brighton Valley will want to adopt them. Can you ask around? You might talk to the minister. He'd probably be a good resource."

"That's an idea. I'll see what I can do."

As the organist began to play, Jason nudged Braden's arm. "That's our cue. Come on, let's go."

They walked into the church along the altar and stopped where the Reverend Steuben had instructed them to stand. Then they faced the wedding guests.

Jason's new family sat in the front row. Karen Bailey, who'd soon be his mother-in-law, had told him to call her Mom. He hadn't done so yet, but something told him it wouldn't be long before the good-hearted woman made it seem like the most natural thing in the world for him to do. Next to her sat Jolene Crenshaw, otherwise known as Gram. The spunky old gal was proving to be a real hoot, with stories he might never tire of hearing. Then there was Braden's mom, Shannon Miller. The sweet lady had reached out to Jason years ago, but he hadn't accepted her friendship when he'd been a boy. Things were different now.

He'd grown up—especially these past few weeks. He had a sister and brother he hadn't appreciated until now. And if they were willing, he'd like to get to know them better.

As the organist changed the tune to the bridal march, Carly started down the aisle. His sister had grown into a beautiful young woman. He hoped that she hadn't been as damaged by her parents as he'd been by his. But if so, Jason hoped she found someone special someday, a loving man who touched her heart and soul like Juliana had touched his.

While Carly took her place along the altar, Juliana proceeded down the aisle. His beautiful bride, dressed in a gown of white, nearly stole his breath away. She held a bouquet in front of her belly, where their daughter grew. But she wasn't hiding her secret. Not any longer. They were going to be parents, and his name would join hers on the baby's birth certificate.

As Juliana approached the altar, Jason reached out to her, and she placed her hand in his.

This was it. The day his life would change.

No—the day his life would truly begin.

"Dearly beloved," Reverend Steuben said as he started the ceremony.

Jason could scarcely hear the words. All he could think of was how lucky he was, how glad he was to make Juliana his wife—forever, from this day forward—until death parted them.

Jason hadn't spared any expense when he'd booked the honeymoon suite at The St. Regis in Houston and lined up their catering staff. From the time the valet opened the passenger door until the newlyweds had been escorted to their room, Juliana and Jason were treated like royalty.

Soft music welcomed them into their elegantly decorated suite, where several bouquets of long-stemmed red roses adorned the living area. Platters of chocolate truffles, fresh fruit and a variety of cheeses, as well as a silver champagne bucket and two crystal flutes, sat on the glass-topped table.

"This is amazing," Juliana said.

Jason brushed a kiss on her cheek, then tipped the bellman.

"Why, thank you, sir." After placing their luggage in the dressing room, the bellman stood at the door. "If there's anything you need, Mr. Rayburn, don't hesitate to ask."

Juliet couldn't imagine what that might be, unless he planned to order their dinner from room service.

When they were finally alone, she looked at the ice bucket, which held two bottles rather than one. She placed her hand on her baby bump. "I'm not able to have champagne. Are you going to drink both of those?"

Jason gripped the neck of one bottle and lifted out sparkling apple cider. "I thought we should both toast our marriage tonight."

She placed her hands on her hips and smiled. "Why, Mr. Rayburn. You've turned out to be far more romantic than I realized."

He tossed her a crooked grin. "Should I apologize?"

She moved toward him and slipped her arms around his neck. "Don't you dare. I love romance—and I especially love *you*." Then she kissed him, long and deep.

As their bodies pressed together, Jason's hands slid along the curve of her back and down the slope of her derriere. He pulled her hips forward, against his erection, showing her how badly he wanted her.

She whimpered, then arched forward, revealing her own need, her own arousal.

When she thought she was going to die from desire, she ended the kiss, then slowly turned and lifted her hair, silently asking him to unzip her gown.

As Jason slid Juliana's zipper down in a slow and deliberate fashion, he slipped the fabric over her shoulders and let it fall to the floor. Then he kissed the back of her neck.

Moments later, she turned and stood before him in a white lace bra and matching panties. Her body, petite yet lithe, was everything he'd imagined it to be and more. Even the rounded slope of her belly, where their daughter grew, made her more feminine, more lovely. More alluring.

Today she became his wife, his life partner. And tonight, she had become his lover.

Following her lead, he undressed, too. When he'd removed all but his shorts, he eased toward her.

She skimmed her nails across his chest, sending a shiver through his veins and a rush of heat through his blood. Then she unsnapped her bra and freed her breasts, full and round, the dusky pink tips peaked.

As he bent and took a nipple in his mouth, she gasped in pleasure. He lavished first one breast, and then the other. Fully aroused, she swayed and clutched his shoulder to stay balanced.

Taking her gently in his arms, he carried her to the bedroom and placed her on top of the white goose-down comforter. Her luscious red curls splayed upon the pillow. Never had a woman appeared so lovely, so tempting...

Jason wanted nothing more than to slip out of his shorts and feel her skin against his, but he paused for a beat, drinking in the angelic sight.

"You're beautiful," he said, the words coming out in near reverence. Then he joined her on the bed, where they continued to kiss, to taste and to stroke each other until they were desperate for more.

"I want to feel you inside me," she said, pulling free of his embrace. "We can take things slow later. We have all night."

He didn't want to prolong the foreplay any longer, either. And she was right. They not only had the rest of the night, they had a lifetime ahead of them.

As he hovered over her, she reached for his erection and guided him home.

He entered her slowly, getting the feel of her, the feel of them. And as her body responded to his, she arched up to meet each of his thrusts, their pleasure mounting.

It seemed as though the world around them stood still—the universe, too. Nothing mattered but the two of them and what they were feeling and sharing together.

When Juliana reached a peak, she cried out, arched her back and let go. He released with her in an explosion that left him seeing a blast of comets and swirling stars.

As they lay on the rumpled comforter, lost in the magic of all they felt for each other, they listened to the music in the background, songs that promised true love would last forever.

When their breathing slowed and their heart rates returned to a steady beat, Jason ran his hand along the slope of her womb. "I can't wait until the baby is big enough for me to feel her move."

"At the rate she's growing, that shouldn't be too long.

He smiled. "It's exciting. I can't wait to see her, to hold her."

"What do you think we should we call her?" Juliana asked.

"Would you mind if we named her after Granny? Not Rosabelle, which doesn't sound very modern. But maybe Rose or Belle?"

"How about Bella Rose?" Juliana asked.

"I like that. It's a pretty name—for a little princess."

As they snuggled together, Jason drew Juliana close, savoring the way she fit in his arms, the softness of her skin, the light fragrance of her floral perfume.

"You know," he said, "I used to be afraid of getting this close to someone else."

"Physically?" she asked.

"No, that's not what I mean. It's not about sexual closeness. Strangers can do that."

She placed her hand along his cheek and smiled. "I know exactly what you mean." Then she trailed her fingers down to his heart. "It's a feeling that runs much deeper than sex."

"That's what I was getting at. And now that I have

you, I can't imagine being the loner I used to be. What would I do without you in my life, Juliana?"

"Grow to be a lonely old man?"

"That's true. What an awful thought."

She smiled. "Just think. You no longer have to worry about being lonely. Today you became a husband and father in one fell swoop."

"Don't forget, I also became a son and a grandson. My small family grew exponentially when I married you."

"That's true. I hope you're prepared for what that's going to mean."

"Life won't be boring," he said.

"That's for sure."

"But I didn't expect it to be. Thank you for making my life complete."

Then he kissed his wife again, knowing that he'd spend the rest of his life trying to make her as happy as she'd made him.

* * * * *

Don't miss Carly Rayburn's story,
the next installment of
BRIGHTON VALLEY COWBOYS
the new miniseries by
USA TODAY *bestselling author Judy Duarte.*
Coming soon to Harlequin Special Edition!

REQUEST YOUR FREE BOOKS!

2 FREE NOVELS PLUS 2 FREE GIFTS!

H HARLEQUIN®

SPECIAL EDITION

Life, Love & Family

HSE15

Marco Palermo is convinced Jordyn Garrett is The One for him. But it'll be a challenge to convince the beautiful brunette to open her heart to him—and the happily-ever-after only he can give her!

Read on for a sneak preview of
THE BACHELOR TAKES A BRIDE, the latest book in
Brenda Harlen's *popular miniseries,*
THOSE ENGAGING GARRETTS!:
THE CAROLINA COUSINS.

He settled his hands lightly on her hips, holding her close but not too tight. He wanted her to know that this was her choice while leaving her in no doubt about what he wanted. She pressed closer to him, and the sensation of her soft curves against his body made him ache.

He parted her lips with his tongue and she opened willingly. She tasted warm and sweet—with a hint of vanilla from the coffee she'd drank—and the exquisite flavor of her spread through his blood, through his body, like an addictive drug.

He felt something bump against his shin. Once. Twice.

The cat, he realized, in the same moment he decided he didn't dare ignore its warning.

Not that he was afraid of Gryffindor, but he was afraid of scaring off Jordyn. Beneath her passionate response, he sensed a lingering wariness and uncertainty.

Slowly, reluctantly, he eased his lips from hers.

She drew in an unsteady breath, confusion swirling in her deep green eyes when she looked at him. "What… what just happened here?"

"I think we just confirmed that there's some serious chemistry between us."

She shook her head. "I'm not going to go out with you, Marco."

There was a note of something—almost like panic—in her voice that urged him to proceed cautiously. "I don't mind staying in," he said lightly.

She choked on a laugh. "I'm not going to have sex with you, either."

"Not tonight," he agreed. "I'm not *that* easy."

This time, she didn't quite manage to hold back the laugh, though sadness lingered in her eyes.

"You have a great laugh," he told her.

Her gaze dropped and her smile faded. "I haven't had much to laugh about in a while."

"Are you ever going to tell me about it?"

He braced himself for one of her flippant replies, a deliberate brush-off, and was surprised by her response.

"Maybe," she finally said. "But not tonight."

It was an acknowledgment that she would see him again, and that was enough for now.

Don't miss
THE BACHELOR TAKES A BRIDE
by Brenda Harlen,
available September 2015 wherever
Harlequin® Special Edition books and ebooks are sold.

www.Harlequin.com